'Could I fire  you believe I

He was standing  throbbing, taunted by the languorous look in her heavy-lidded eyes.

'You'd hardly want to,' she said, and although she spoke lightly, he guessed she, too, was trapped by a sudden shift in the atmosphere in the room. 'I mean, look at me—your archetypal Plain Jane! I'm jeans and T-shirt, not high fashion—short and dumpy, not slim and willowy.'

'You're a woman, and I'm a man,' he said, determined to prove his point, although somewhere deep inside he was distressed she should make light of her appearance. 'Sometimes that is all it takes.'

He took her hand and drew her to her feet, not forcing her, but allowing no resistance, and then made the kiss a reality, his lips claiming hers with an arrogance that took her breath away.

MEDITERRANEAN DOCTORS

Let these exotic doctors sweep you off your feet...

**Be tantalised by their smouldering good-looks,
romanced by their fiery passion, and
warmed by the emotional power
of these strong and caring men...**

MEDITERRANEAN DOCTORS

Passionate about life, love and medicine.

THE SPANISH DOCTOR'S CONVENIENT BRIDE

BY

MEREDITH WEBBER

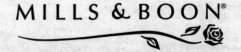

MILLS & BOON®

First published in Great Britain 2006
Paperback edition 2007
Harlequin Mills & Boon Limited,
Eton House, 18-24 Paradise Road, Richmond, Surrey TW9 1SR

© Meredith Webber 2006

ISBN-13: 978 0 263 85223 3
ISBN-10:   0 263 85223 7

Set in Times Roman 10½ on 12¾ pt
03-0207-50945

Printed and bound in Spain
by Litografia Rosés, S.A., Barcelona

Meredith Webber says of herself, 'Some years ago, I read an article which suggested that Mills & Boon® were looking for new medical authors. I had one of those "I can do that" moments, and gave it a try. What began as a challenge has become an obsession, though I do temper the "butt on seat" career of writing with dirty but healthy outdoor pursuits, fossicking through the Australian Outback in search of gold or opals. Having had some success in all of these endeavours, I now consider I've found the perfect lifestyle.'

Recent titles by the same author:

A FATHER BY CHRISTMAS
BRIDE AT BAY HOSPITAL
THE DOCTOR'S MARRIAGE WISH
  Crocodile Creek: 24-Hour Rescue
SHEIKH SURGEON

CHAPTER ONE

'MOZART would be good for all the babies in the NICU,' Marty protested. 'I've picked out melodies everyone knows so the parents would enjoy it too. Besides, Emmaline is used to it. It's what I've played for her all along.'

Sophie Gibson touched her friend lightly on the shoulder.

'She's not your baby,' she gently reminded Marty. 'In fact, she's not even called Emmaline.'

'But you've got to admit she looks like an Emmaline, doesn't she?'

Marty put her hand through the port of the humidi-crib and touched the wild black hair poking up from beneath the stockingette cap on the head of the tiny baby. Emmaline's cherub face was screwed up as if sleeping required the utmost concentration, her little fists tucked up against her chin, ready to take on anyone who bothered her.

Or who messed with her Mozart!

'She looks like a baby,' Sophie said, then turned, smiling, as she heard her husband's voice.

'Glad you're both here,' Alexander Gibson said quietly. 'Sophie, Marty, I'd like you both to meet Dr Carlos Quintero. He's the baby's father.'

Gib's eyes sought out Marty, and she hoped the sick despair that squeezed her stomach wasn't written on her face.

Stupid to have grown attached to Emmaline—stupid, stupid, stupid!

'Carlos, this is Sophie Gibson, second in charge of the neonatal intensive care unit, and Marty Cox, the obstetrician who took care of Natalie during the time she was in on life support in the intensive care unit.'

The dark-haired, deeply tanned stranger bowed his head towards the two women, but Marty sensed his eyes, hidden beneath hooded, jet-fringed lids, were on Emm—the baby.

Then he lifted his head and eyes as dark as his lashes—obsidian stones in his harsh-planed face—met Marty's.

'I will wish to speak further to you,' he said, his deep, accented voice, though quiet, carrying easily around the room.

Presence, that's what he has, Marty thought, although she doubted presence was the reason for a sudden fluttery feeling in her chest.

'Of course,' she agreed, as easily as possible given the fluttery stuff going on. 'Any time. Well, not quite any time, but we can make a time.'

She was chattering, something she only did when she was nervous, and of course Emmaline's father suddenly turning up would make her nervous.

Wouldn't it?

'Why not now?' Sophie suggested. 'You've just come off duty.'

Marty fired a 'some friend you are' glance towards the neonatologist, and wondered just how bad she, herself, looked.

Flat hair from the cap she'd been wearing in the delivery room, a too-large scrub suit billowing around her slight frame.

And you're worrying because? her inner voice demanded.

'You'd probably prefer to spend time with the baby right now,' she mumbled at the stranger, who cast a look towards the crib then turned back to Marty.

'Not at all. Now would suit me if it is convenient for you.'

Marty looked helplessly towards Sophie, who had to hide the smile, while Gib made matters worse by suggesting they use his office, which had a super coffee-maker and comfortable armchairs in which they could sit.

'You know how to work the coffee-machine,' he reminded Marty as she dragged her reluctant body out of the NICU, far too aware of the tall dark stranger following behind her.

'Talk about a cliché!' she muttered to herself as this description of Carlos whoever flashed through her mind.

'I am sorry?'

She turned and shrugged.

'No, *I'm* sorry. Talking to myself. Bad habit.'

'And one I also have,' the polite doctor informed her. 'Though, in my case, I am often the only person who understands me.'

'You can say that again!' Marty told him, turning to smile as she added, 'Though there are times when even I don't understand me.'

'Ah!' He returned her smile, brilliant white teeth flashing in his dark face, deep lines creasing the tanned cheeks and crinkling the skin at the corner of his eyes. 'But that is more than a language problem, is it not?'

Still getting over the effect of the smile—which had stuck her feet to the floor and made her stomach swoop in a wild roller-coaster simulation—she had no idea what to say to this fairly acute observation.

She settled on a lame 'Gib's office is through here' and led the way along the corridor and into the comfortable room. At least, while she busied herself at the coffee-machine she wouldn't have to look at this Carlos—wouldn't have to see the silver strands in his night-dark hair, or the smooth tanned skin stretched over hard muscle in his arms, or the way his fine-boned nose seemed to direct the eye towards sinfully shapely lips.

And how come she'd noticed that much? She who looked on men as necessary adjuncts to the continuation of the species and, at best, useful friends who could reach the highest shelves in the supermarket or lift things down from on top of cupboards?

She shook her head as the espresso machine delivered its final drops into the two small cups, took a deep breath and turned back to find the man studying the photos of some of Gib's patients that adorned the walls of his office.

'You call these before and after photos?' he said, turning as she put the coffee cups on the low table. 'I have never done much neonatology. It is amazing to think these small babies can grow into such sturdy children and healthy-looking teenagers.'

'They get the best possible start in this NICU,' Marty told him. 'With Emmaline—I'm sorry, with your baby we weren't sure how premature she was, but her birth weight was 1500 grams, which put her into low birth weight category. So she'd have gone there rather than the other nursery anyway. In the NICU she can be watched every minute of the day in case any of the things that beset premmie babies crops up.'

Had he noticed her slip?

He didn't mention it, settling himself in a chair near the table and spooning sugar into his coffee.

'Emmaline?' Dark eyebrows rose as he said the word and Marty squirmed with embarrassment.

'I know it's silly, but I've kind of known her, you see, right from when Natalie was admitted. I was called to consult in A and E when she was brought in after the accident, and then when the decision was made to keep her on life support for the baby's sake, I was the obstetrician in charge—but Gib's already told you that part. The hospital couldn't track down any relatives, which meant Natalie had no visitors so there was no one to talk to the baby. I used to visit, and talk to it, and play music—'

'Mozart?'

So he had heard her conversation. She really should learn to argue more quietly. But playing Mozart had been little enough to do for the baby and the brain-dead woman who had been carrying her, so she tilted her chin and defended her actions.

'Did you know a researcher once had a group of adolescents take a test, then played some Mozart for them, then had them take a parallel test and every one of them did better? I don't know if it made any difference to the baby, or to Natalie, but it's beautiful music. I love Bach—probably more than Mozart—but I thought he might be too complex for the baby, so stuck with a lot of the piano concertos—'

She stopped abruptly as embarrassment coiled and writhed like something alive inside her.

'Of course, my musical tastes are nothing to do with what you want to know, which was—'

Marty had no idea where the conversation had begun, so she picked up her coffee and took a gulp. Quite dreadful—she'd forgotten to put sugar in, or was too muddled to have given it a thought.

'Emmaline,' he repeated, and she felt embarrassment heat her body as she remembered.

'I didn't name her right away. I called her "the baby" or just "baby" when I visited for the four weeks Natalie was in the ICU, but then, when I delivered her, she was a tiny scrap of humanity with this wealth of black hair.' She smiled. 'I'd had a doll with hair like that when I was young and she was Emmaline, so the name just sort of stuck.'

'Emmaline Quintero!' He spoke as if tasting the name on his tongue, and Marty, wondering if there was a word that would convey the ultimate in mortification—mortifiedest?—rushed into speech again.

'You don't have to call her Emmaline, of course you don't. You'll have your own name for her, a family name maybe—your mother's name—a favourite, or you could call her after Natalie.'

Big mistake! The man's face became a mask of nothingness, all expression wiped away—black eyes boring into Marty's, lips thinned and tight as he said coldly, 'I think not.'

Do *not* apologise, Marty's inner voice ordered, but she was beyond help from within and had already rushed into a confused bout of 'sorrys'.

'The decision to keep Natalie on life support? That was yours?'

Thankfully, Carlos's question cut across her stumbling apologies and Marty was able to grasp the lifeline of a purely medical question.

Although why was he questioning the decision?

Refusing to think about the implications of that one, Marty explained.

'Actually, in the absence of any relative that we could contact, the hospital ethics committee made the decision. They went on the advice of the neonatologist—Sophie was the one consulted at the time—and my judgement of the stage of the pregnancy. It was deemed advisable, for the baby's sake—'

'What was that judgement?'

Marty was prepared to accept his interruption—after all, the man had stuff he wanted to know—but the cold, hard voice in which he interrupted—she didn't like that one little bit.

'My judgement of the stage of pregnancy?' she queried, her voice as cold and hard as his—all compassion gone. Two could play this game. 'I measured fundal height, and used ultrasound to estimate the length of the baby and head circumference. But although these measurements are fairly close in the first and second trimester, by the third, beginning at twenty-eight weeks—'

Too much information now—he'd know all this medical detail—but he didn't interrupt so she kept going.

'They can be out by as much as three weeks, and that's plus or minus. The man who was in the car gave no help apart to say she was pregnant when she moved in with him so the closest we could get was twenty-eight to thirty-one weeks. Natalie was tall and slim so it was also possible the pregnancy could have been further along than that—a possibility that became a probability when Em—the baby—was delivered.'

'*Dios*! Call the baby Emmaline if you wish. Anything is better than this stumbling every time she's mentioned.' He glared at Marty, as if defying her to disobey his order, then demanded, 'So, if anything, Natalie was further into her pregnancy than your initial assessment—that *is* what you're saying?'

Marty nodded, feeling sorry now for Emmaline who had this disagreeable man for a father.

'And the man said she was pregnant when she returned to him?'

'I don't know about "returned". He said she was already pregnant when she came and that's all he'd say.'

'Oh, she returned, for sure,' Carlos told her, enough ice in his voice to make Marty shiver.

There was a long silence, then he added, 'So this Emmaline, she *is* mine!'

He ground out the words with such evident regret—distaste almost—Marty let fly.

'You make it sound as if she's an albatross hung around your neck by some malign fate. She's a baby—she's not to blame for being born. You're a doctor—you of all people know how conception happens. Actually, ten-year-old kids know how it happens these days. But it was up to you. If you didn't want a child, you should have done something to prevent it.'

She was glaring directly at him so caught the flash of something that might be humour in his eyes, then he smiled as he said, 'And do you always think of the possibility of conception when you make love with your partner? Or is the easing of the urgent need the priority of both mind and body?'

The smile, though as coolly cynical as the words, confused her to the extent she forgot to breathe, then, angry at her reaction, she snapped at him.

'I don't have a partner!'

Oh, hell! Mortification all over again because that

wasn't the issue—her personal life was none of Carlos Quintero's business.

Fine, dark eyebrows rose again and the jet-black eyes seemed to penetrate her scrub suit to scan the body hidden beneath it.

Infuriated beyond reason, Marty stood up, grabbed the empty cups off the table and carried them across the room. This man wasn't interested in his wife, or how she'd died. His only concern—hope?—had been that maybe the baby wasn't his.

Callous, arrogant wretch, with his insinuating remarks and come-to-bed eyes scanning her body!

'It is not for myself I regret Emmaline,' he said, and Marty's wrath, which had been building up nicely, dissipated instantly. He'd used her name! 'It is she I am thinking of. The life I lead—it is no life for a baby, yet it is work to which I am committed. This is hard, you see, for me now to have a baby and to know what best to do with it.'

'Her,' Marty corrected automatically.

'Her!' he repeated obediently.

Carlos watched the woman's shoulders slump and knew he'd won a reprieve. He, who hated above all things to be dependent on another person, needed help—help to understand what had happened, and where things stood—help to work out what to do next. And one thing was clear— this woman had the baby's—Emmaline's—interest at heart and for that reason, he guessed, she might be willing to help a stranger.

She returned to her chair, though he could read her reluctance in the way she moved and her distrust in the way she held her body. One of those women to whom their job is their life, he guessed, though her attachment to the baby was strange—professional detachment usually went hand in hand with such dedication.

'Do you know any details of the accident?' he asked, steering the conversation away from the baby in the hope she might relax a little.

'Only that it was single vehicle—apparently the car careened off the road on a curve and struck a tree—and Natalie was breathing on her own when the ambulance arrived. She stopped breathing when she was moved and they revived her twice at the site then put her on life support to bring her to the hospital. Foetal heart rate was stable throughout the examinations, and tests at the hospital showed no damage to the amniotic sac or the placenta and, as far as we could tell, no damage to the foetus.'

'And the man?'

He saw the woman's quick glance—clear, almond-shaped, hazel eyes sweeping across his face—before she replied.

'Multiple fractures to both legs, some contusions and concussion, I think a ruptured spleen but nothing life-threatening.'

A shame, Carlos thought, then dismissed the thought as petty and unworthy. It wasn't Peter Richards's fault Natalie had loved him. Although, if he'd not broken off their engagement, sending her scurrying to Europe to forget him, the beautiful blonde would never have crossed Carlos's path and this entire, unsatisfactory mess could have been avoided.

Though he wouldn't use the words 'unsatisfactory mess' to this fiery little obstetrician!

Marty—as strange a name as Emmaline!

'So he was hospitalised here?'

Marty nodded, though the look on her face suggested she was no more fond of Peter Richards than he was.

'You didn't like him?'

'I didn't know him, but I do know, once he was mobile, he never visited her, to sit with her and talk to her. I know she'd been ruled brain-dead but no one knows if on some deep level such people might feel comfort or support. He should have done it for his own sake if nothing else—having survived the accident that killed her—but he didn't even come to say his goodbyes. She lay there, all alone, and so beautiful it hurt to look at her.'

Carlos saw his companion's lips tighten to a thin line as she described what she saw as Peter Richards's shortcomings. But she was right, Natalie *had* been beautiful. So beautiful she'd bewitched him, and he'd pursued her with an ardour and determination he'd never felt before, though beautiful women hadn't been lacking in his life.

Anger stirred briefly—directed not at Peter Richards for his behaviour, or at Natalie for not loving him, but at himself for his folly in wanting her anyway, then he dismissed it, for the matter at hand was the baby.

A tap on the door, then a nurse popped her head around the jamb.

'Dr Quintero, I'm about to change the baby and feed her. Would you like to see her? Hold her?'

He could feel Marty's eyes on him but refused to look her way.

'Not this time,' he said, then felt obliged to make an excuse. 'I have flown halfway around the world through too many time zones and am tired enough to maybe drop her.'

The nurse disappeared and he was unable to avoid

turning back to Marty, who watched him, one mobile eyebrow raised in his direction.

'What can I do with a baby?' he demanded, so irritated by her attitude he was practically growling.

'Bring it up?' she suggested, and now he did growl.

'You know nothing of my life. You sit there, so prim and righteous, passing judgement on Peter Richards, passing judgement on me. I work in Sudan, among people who lose their babies every day, so wretched is their existence. Children die because I cannot save them, because they have had nothing but stones to eat, and their mothers are so malnourished they cannot feed them. They might walk as long as six days to seek treatment for themselves or their children, then leave our small, makeshift hospital and walk back home again. *That* is my life!'

Marty was sorry she'd prodded. Like most people, she was overwhelmed with helplessness when she considered the death and destruction in famine- or war-ravaged countries. But that didn't alter the fact that Emmaline was this man's child. His responsibility.

'So this baby doesn't count?' she persisted, and he stood up and paced around the room, a tall, angry stranger with a face that might be carved from teak, so strongly were his bones delineated beneath his skin, so remote the expression on those graven features.

'I will deal with the baby!' he said, after several minutes of pacing. 'I come because a message reaches me—my wife is injured, dying perhaps. Do you think she told me she was pregnant before she left me? Do you think I would have let her go, carrying my baby? The baby is news when I reach the hospital. What am I supposed to do—summon up a carer for a baby out of thin air? Make plans for what school she will attend?'

'I'm sorry!' This time Marty's apology was heart-felt. 'I didn't realise you hadn't known. It must have been terrible for you—to arrive and learn you had a child. Most people have nine months to get used to the idea—to make plans. But you don't have to decide anything immediately. Sophie wants to keep Emmaline in for at least another fortnight. At best, she was a month premature and her birth weight was very low, so she's vulnerable to all the complications of both premmie and low birth weight infants.'

'But so far, has had none of them?'

'She was jaundiced after two days but that's common enough and phototherapy cleared it up. Gib told you she's five days old?'

Carlos nodded.

'I assume Natalie's deteriorating condition made a Caesar necessary earlier, possibly, than you would have liked?'

'Her organs were shutting down,' Marty agreed. 'Life-support machines can only do so much. For Emmaline's sake, it was advisable to operate.'

'So now we have a baby.'

Marty would have liked to correct him—to say *he* had a baby—but he'd spoken quietly, as if moving towards acceptance, and she didn't want to antagonise him again. In the meantime, she was missing Emmaline's feeding time and a subtle ache in her arms reminded her of how much she'd been enjoying her contact with the little girl—*and* how unprofessional her behaviour was to have allowed herself to grow so attached.

She'd chosen to specialise in O and G rather than paediatrics so this didn't happen—so she wouldn't be forever getting clucky over other people's children. In O and G you took care of the woman, delivered the baby, and after one postnatal check the family was gone from your life, or at least until the next pregnancy.

But with Emmaline it hadn't worked that way, and all the up-till-then successfully repressed maternal urges had come bursting forth and Marty, doomed to childlessness, had fallen in love with a tiny scrap of humanity with a scrunched-up face, a putty nose, let-me-at-them fists and jet-black hair.

Misery swamped her, providing a partial antidote to the flutters she still felt when she looked at Emmaline's father.

Get with it, woman, the inner voice ordered, and Marty tried.

'I should be going,' she said, standing up, acting positive and in control, but still waiting until his pacing took him away from the door before heading in that direction herself.

Just in case the antidote wasn't working…

He moved a different way, blocking her path.

'I've kept you from your dinner. Do you have far to go to your home?'

Politeness?

Or did he want more from her?

Positive! In control!

'Dinner can wait,' she said lightly, waving her hand in the air in case he hadn't picked up the nonchalance in her voice. 'And, no, my home's not far. Walking distance actually. I live in an apartment by the river in a parkland area called South Bank.'

Explaining too much again, but the antidote wasn't working—not at all—and the man's proximity—his body standing so close to hers—was affecting her again, making her feel shaky and uncertain and a lot of other things she hadn't felt for so long it was hard to believe she was feeling them now.

'South Bank? The hospital administrator to whom I spoke earlier was kind enough to book me into a hotel at South Bank. You know of this hotel?'

Only because it's across the road from my apartment building! How's that for fickle fate?

'I know it,' she said cautiously.

'Then, perhaps you will be so kind as to wait while I collect my backpack then guide me on my way.'

He was a visitor to her country so she could hardly refuse, and to flee in desperate disorder down the corridor might look a tad strange.

'Where's your backpack?'

'It is in the office on the ground floor, behind the desk where people enquire about patients or ask for directions. A kind woman on the desk offered to look after it for me.'

'Of course she would,' Marty muttered, then she remembered this man had super-sensitive hearing and was wise to mutterings. She'd better stop doing it forthwith.

'I've got to change so I'll meet you in the foyer,' she suggested, leading the way out of Gib's office and along the corridor to a bank of staff lifts. 'If you turn left when you come out on the ground floor, you'll find the information desk without any trouble.'

Positive! In control!

She was moving away, intending to sneak a few minutes in the NICU before changing—not one hundred per cent in control—when his hand touched her shoulder and she froze.

'Thank you,' he said, though whether his gratitude was

for her directions, her explanations or her kindness to his daughter, Marty had no idea. He'd lifted his hand off her shoulder almost as soon as it had touched down, and then stepped into the lift and disappeared behind the silently closing doors.

They collected his backpack and she led him out of the hospital, into the soft, dark, late January night. Humidity wrapped around them as they walked beneath the vivid bougainvillea that twined above the path through the centre of the park, while the smell of the river wafted through the air.

Usually, this walk was special to Marty, separating as it did her work life from her social life—if going to the occasional concert, learning Mandarin and practising Tae Kwon Do could be called a social life.

But tonight the peace of the walk was disturbed by the company, her body, usually obedient to her demands, behaving badly. It skittered when Carlos brushed his arm against her hip, and nerves leapt beneath her skin when he held her elbow to guide her out of the path of a couple of in-line skaters. If this was attraction, it was unlike anything she'd ever experienced before, and if it wasn't attraction, then what the hell was it?

She was too healthy for it to be the start of some contagion, but surely too old, not to mention too sensible, to be feeling the lustful urges of an adolescent towards a total stranger.

'This is my apartment block and your hotel is there, across the road.'

Given how she was reacting to him, it was the sensible thing to do but as she stood there, banishing this tired, bereaved, confused man to the anonymity of a hotel room, she felt a sharp pang of guilt, as if her mother was standing behind her, prodding her with the tip of a carving knife.

'You'll be OK?' she asked, then immediately regretted it. He couldn't possibly be all right after all he'd been through. But he let her off the hook, nodding acquiescence.

'I will see you again,' he said, before shifting the weight of his backpack against his shoulders and crossing the road to the hotel, a tall dark shadow in the streetlights—a man who walked alone.

She turned towards her apartment building, free to mutter now, castigating herself for feeling sorry for him, but also warning him, in his absence, that the 'seeing you again' scenario was most unlikely.

Emmaline had a family now—there'd be no need for her to provide that special contact all babies needed. Emmaline's father was best placed to do this for her and it was up to him to decide where the little one's future lay.

Her heart might ache as she accepted these truths, but it was time to be sensible and make a clean break from the baby who had sneaked beneath her guard and professionalism, and had wormed her way into her heart.

She rode the lift up to her floor, then opened the apartment door, walking through the darkened rooms to stand on the balcony and look out at the river, reminding herself of all the positives in her life—a job she loved, a great apartment, interests and friends—but neither the river nor her thoughts filled the aching emptiness within her, and she hugged herself tightly as she went back inside to find something for her dinner.

CHAPTER TWO

'I MAY join you?'

Had he been watching for her that she'd barely left her apartment when Carlos appeared by her side? A shiver ran down Marty's spine, not because he *might* have been watching but because of the way his voice curled into her ears.

She turned to look at him in daylight—to see if a night's sleep had softened the hard angles of his face. If anything they were sharper, while the skin beneath his eyes was darkly shadowed. The man looked more strained than he had the previous day.

Not that dark shadows under his eyes made any difference to her internal reaction to the man. Looking at him caused more tremors along her nerves than listening to him.

Determined to hide these wayward reactions, she went for professional.

'Didn't sleep much?' she diagnosed, and saw a flicker of a smile.

'The hotel is comfortable, but there was much to think about, and air-conditioned air—how do people sleep in it?'

Marty took it as a rhetorical question and didn't try to explain that for a lot of people it was the only way they *could* sleep in the hot, humid summer.

The major question was, why was he here?

Had his sleepless night convinced him of his responsibilities?

Could he be interested enough in his daughter to be visiting her at seven in the morning?

'You're going to the hospital?'

'I am.'

Maybe everything *would* work out for Emmaline! But Marty had barely registered her delight for the baby when he squelched it with his next statement.

'I arranged things when I spoke to the administrator. For the next month I will be working there. Not for money, but for useful things to take back with me—equipment the hospital no longer uses because it has been superseded. No equipment is too old-fashioned for us as long as it works.'

The information about the equipment was interesting and she'd have liked to ask what kind of things he found most useful, knowing there were store-cupboards full of obstetrics gear that no one ever used tucked away at the hospital.

But something he'd said at the beginning of the conversation needed following up before she started donating old bedpans.

'Working at the hospital? I'm sure if you asked they'd give you whatever they didn't need anyway, so why would you want to work? Haven't you heard of holidays?'

And shouldn't you be spending your time getting to know your daughter—making arrangements for her care?

'I try to work at other hospitals whenever I'm on leave, but not only in the hope of getting some useful equipment. My specialty is surgery and I have plenty of accident experience but there is always a time when I realise how little I know and when I wish I'd learnt more of other specialties. Your own field, obstetrics, is one of my weaknesses. Oh, I can do the basics but in Sudan I'm not needed for basics. There, the women look after each other and have good midwives, so mainly I'm needed for emergencies and this is where I fail my patients.'

'You can hardly be held responsible for failing patients with complicated obstetrics problems,' Marty told him. 'Even obstetricians do that at times.'

'I should know more,' he said, refusing her excuses. 'So, at the hospital I will work in the A and E Department and take the obstetrics patients, assisting, of course, a specialist such as yourself.'

Great! Flickering along her nerves she could put up with if it only happened occasionally, and was time-limited—like for a day or two! But a month? When he'd be around all the time?

Maybe she'd get over it.

She sneaked a look towards him, catching his profile as he turned to watch a pelican skid to a landing on the river's surface, and knew she probably wouldn't get over it. Whatever was happening inside her body was getting worse, not better, which was weird to say the least, because she wasn't sure she even liked the man.

'And Emmaline?' she asked, knowing if anything was going to put her off him, his attitude to his child surely would.

'I will have a month to think about the situation. As you said, the doctors want to keep her in for another fortnight, so the need to do something isn't urgent. At the moment— well, at the moment I don't know.'

His voice told her the subject was closed, but this was Emmaline, so as far as Marty was concerned it had to be reopened.

'Don't know if you want her, or don't know what to do with her?' she persisted.

'How could I *want* her? I knew nothing of her existence! And a baby—it is impossible to fit a baby in my life. But she is my responsibility and I will make such arrangements as I see fit!'

'She's a child, not a responsibility!' Marty muttered, forgetting that muttering was out.

And he did hear her, for he turned towards her, his face harsh with anger.

'You are wrong, Marty Cox, and you are allowing emotion to cloud your thinking. A child must be the greatest responsibility a person can have.'

'You're right as far as that goes,' Marty conceded, 'but surely a child is a responsibility that should be considered with love, not just as a duty. Emotion *has* to come into it.'

'*Never*!' he argued, his deep voice rolling out the word with such certainty Marty frowned at him. 'Emotion clouds too many issues—it makes us stupid, that's what emotion does. A parent would be neglectful if he allowed emotion to sway the decisions or arrangements he makes for his child. He would be irresponsible.'

Was that true?

Should emotion be set aside in responsible decision-making?

Surely not, when how you feel about something at a gut level should always count in a decision. And wasn't gut-level thinking emotion?

But, then, how could she, who had no child, argue that point?

'As you say, you have a couple of weeks,' she said lamely.

They walked on in silence, Marty perturbed enough by

his 'emotionless arrangements' idea to barely notice the way her body was behaving.

Would his arrangements include putting the baby up for adoption?

How would she fare in the ranks of adoptive parents? A single parent who worked full time? There were so many childless couples out there, and those who could be full-time parents—social workers would surely favour such families for a healthy little baby like Emmaline. And shouldn't she have been on a list?

Her mother would love a grandchild and she'd be happy to mind her while Marty worked.

But surely there was that list of hopeful adoptive parents—a list without the name Marty Cox even at the bottom…

Private adoptions?

She'd read of them, but did they really happen?

She glanced at the man again, but trying to read his face was like trying to read a blank sheet of butcher's paper.

'You are concerned?'

She'd turned away so had to look back at him.

'Concerned?'

'You sighed.'

'I never sigh!'

'Never? Not in the dead of the night when sleep won't come and your thoughts are too confused to be sorted into shape? Not even when people's stupidity creates problems for themselves and others? Why would you not sigh?'

'Because it's defeatist!' Marty snapped, remembering something her mother had told her when she'd been very young and had probably been sighing about the unfair-ness of fate. 'Why bother sighing, when you could be do-ing something about whatever is wrong? And if you can't do anything about it, then again, why sigh? It doesn't achieve anything.'

'But it does release some tension or emotion, does it not?'

'So does Tae Kwon Do, and it has the benefit of keeping you fit at the same time.'

'But you can hardly kick out at your opponent in the operating theatre,' Carlos said, and Marty, hearing something in his voice, turned to see a slight smile on his face.

He was teasing her!

And she didn't like it one bit!

Did she really never sigh, or had she simply been making conversation?

Carlos studied his companion as she strode along, her eyes focussed on the path ahead of them, her thoughts who knew where?

Her slight figure moved briskly—a no-nonsense woman, this Marty Cox—no-nonsense, like her name. No-nonsense hair, cut short to hide, he suspected, a tendency to curl. No-nonsense muddy blonde, not highlighted as so many women wore their hair these days. It feathered around her neat head, a lighter colour at the tips, where it brushed against the almost translucent skin on her temples.

And though slim, she had curves in all the right places, and his body had already registered an attraction.

Not that she'd respond!

No-nonsense through and through would be his judgement, except that her eyes belied it. He remembered them slanting towards him as he'd asked a question—a greenish, bluish colour with gold pinpoints around the pupils. Dreamer's eyes!

He shook his head. The sleepless night could be blamed

for this fantasy, although not for the attraction he felt towards this woman. Had Natalie's princess-like beauty captured Marty's imagination, prompting her deep compassion, her involvement? Was that why she'd taken so much interest in Natalie's baby?

Natalie's baby?

He hadn't thought of the baby that way before.

And wouldn't again if he could help it—the idea distasteful somehow.

As the forthright Marty Cox had pointed out, Emmaline was *his* baby.

But Emmaline?

A fantasy name from the forthright woman?

She was indeed an odd mix.

She was also unclipping her pager from the waist of her jeans.

'Hospital—A and E,' she said briefly, picking up the pace of their progress, taking strides that seemed too long for such a petite woman.

He paced beside her.

'What is your usual procedure with a page? Do you phone in?'

'I would if I was at home, but we're only minutes away now, so I'll be there almost as soon as a phone call. The specialist on night duty must have his hands full for A and E to be paging me.'

They crossed the road and she led the way through a back entrance into the emergency department, lobbing her small backpack onto a shelf behind a manned desk by the door and grabbing a folded scrub suit to pull on over her clothing.

Then, as she thrust her arms into the sleeves, she turned towards him and smiled.

'Well, get yourself ready. We're on!'

Her smile wasn't at all forthright. It was sweet, and slightly shy, as if unrelated to her confident manner and brisk words.

He glanced towards her, hoping she'd smile again, but she was talking to the nurse behind the desk, explaining about the page.

'Oh, it must be the woman in the car they want you for,' the nurse said. 'Her husband's driven into the laundry bay out the back. Let me check.' She leafed through some notes on her desk then explained, 'Full term, breech presentation, feet already out.'

'At least someone had the sense not to try to move her,' Marty replied, then she turned to Carlos. 'Out this way. Have you delivered a breech? Normally it would have been picked up in prenatal care but a lot of women still don't bother with it—or with much of it. When they present here in early labour and we realise it's a breech, we'd do an ultrasound to work out foetal weight, a flat-plate abdomen X-ray to determine if the head is normally flexed or hyper-extended, and we'd do a clinical evaluation of the woman's pelvis. Quite often, if there's time, we can turn the baby. If the baby's too big, or the pelvis is too small, or the head is in the wrong position, we'd consider a Caesar, but with the legs, and by now possibly the body, already delivered, we have to go ahead with a vaginal delivery.'

'I remember the danger in a breech is in the delivery of the head, but you will do this in the car?'

She was snapping on a pair of gloves, but she smiled again, as if pleased he knew that much.

'I imagine if you're doing it back in Sudan it could be in far worse circumstances than the back of a car.'

'Sometimes,' he conceded, 'although where I work there is now a hospital of sorts—the people themselves built it for me, with a thatched roof and mud brick walls, and the people are accepting it and coming if they need help.'

They reached the car and found a nurse kneeling at the open rear door, with a wheelchair, a gurney and several onlookers clustered nearby. The nurse stood up to make room for Marty.

'FHR is strong, the feet showed then retracted but are well out now. I know theoretically about gentle traction on the feet, legs and pelvis in a breech delivery, but what's gentle?'

She introduced Marty to the woman and her husband.

'You've done just fine,' Marty assured the nurse, squatting down so she could say hello to the woman and introduce Carlos, explaining who they both were and what she had to do, then taking hold of the protruding legs and body and slipping the forefinger of her left hand along the baby's back so she could rotate his torso while his shoulders came free.

'It's a gentle pressure,' she explained to Carlos. 'We wait for a contraction, then use a finger to get the shoulder blades free. You're doing really well,' she added to the mother. 'This isn't your first?'

'It's her fifth,' the father replied. 'We had all the others at home but this was a new midwife and she felt the baby was in the wrong position and couldn't turn it so told us to come to the hospital, then, while we were stopped at traffic lights, this happened. My wife had to push and I saw the feet!'

'They'll both be fine,' Marty assured the man, who had obviously been prepared to deliver his child head first but had panicked at seeing feet. She was also reassured herself. After four children the woman's pelvimetry should be flexible enough to expand to release the head. She turned her attention back to the labouring woman. 'You're the boss, so we'll wait until you're ready to push again then rotate him so his arms follow each other out.'

She turned to check the instrument tray, seeing the Piper forceps on it, should she need them to help deliver the head. She'd prefer not to, but if the baby's head was hyper-extended, they'd definitely be needed.

'Now,' the woman gasped, while her husband, who was supporting her, leaned forward over her labouring body to see what was happening.

The arms came free and Marty continued with her instructions to Carlos who stood, bent almost double, beside her.

'Now, with two hands, the left one underneath, you use your forefinger again, only this time you slip it into his mouth to keep his head flexed. Then with the next contraction, we pull down, then lift and pull at the same time. Wait for the push, then—bingo! One brave little boy comes backwards into the world.'

She held him while the nurse wiped his face and gently suctioned his nose and mouth, then handed the baby, who was squalling lustily, to the mother, took a soft towel from the nurse to cover him, then helped move mother and child to a wheelchair so she and the infant could be formally admitted to hospital.

'You don't do an Apgar score straight away?' Carlos asked, and, still smiling about the successful delivery, she turned towards him.

'He cried—that's enough for me. As far as I'm concerned, it's more important for his mother to hold him—to see for herself that he's OK. We'll still get the first Apgar done within a minute—or pretty close to it. Then another at five minutes, but, really, with healthy babies that's stuff to put on charts.'

Their patient was wheeled into one of the trauma rooms in A and E to await the third stage of her labour, and for her new son to be checked out and his birth documented for posterity. But first things first. Marty clamped the cord in two places then handed a pair of surgical scissors to the father so he could cut the cord.

'A son!' the man said, touching the cheek of the baby who was held to his wife's breast.

'A son!' Marty heard Carlos echo, and, turning, saw a look of wonder in his eyes, and although she experienced this same sense of miracle each and every time a new child was born, she had to wonder if he would have felt differently towards Emmaline if he'd been present at her birth.

Or if she'd been a boy?

'Please, no drugs,' the woman said, as Marty gently massaged her abdomen to encourage expulsion of the placenta.

'Providing everything is OK, I'll go along with that,' Marty assured her. 'But you've had a difficult labour and there could be damage to the uterine wall. I won't make any promises at this stage.'

The woman seemed satisfied with this, though it was with reluctance she gave up the baby to be checked, weighed, cleaned and dressed.

'A fine little boy,' Carlos said, when the woman had been admitted—for observation only, Marty had assured her—and the two of them were having a cup of coffee in the staffroom.

The remark reminded Marty of his earlier exclamation and suspicion made her ask, 'Would that have made a difference? To you, I mean? Would it have been different if Emmaline had been a boy?'

He looked genuinely puzzled.

'Why would you think that?'

Marty shrugged.

'Preconceived ideas of Latin men, I suppose. Where are you from? Italy?'

'Spain,' he snapped. 'And on behalf of all so-called Latin men I find your assumption offensive.'

'Do you?' Marty said, challenging him with her eyes. 'I'll retract the Latin bit, if you like, but don't tell me that most men wouldn't prefer at least their firstborn to be a son.'

'Nonsense!' Carlos exploded, so genuinely upset she knew she'd been wrong. So wrong that she held up her hands in surrender.

'OK, I apologise, but from where I sit it was an easy assumption to make. Do you know what Marty's short for? Martina! And, no, I'm not named after a tennis star, but after my father, Martin, who'd wanted a son and when I arrived, the firstborn, named me after himself anyway. I'd like to think that some malign fate is working on the situation but I know it's something to do with his chromosomes. Three marriages and five half-sisters later, he's still without a son. His attitude has skewed things for me.'

She was talking too much again, but the man made her nervous in a way she'd never felt before. She drained her coffee and stood up. She wasn't due on duty for another three-quarters of an hour and it felt like the day was already half-over.

'I have patients to see on the ward then a list of out-patient appointments. Have you met whoever you'll be working under in A and E?'

'Anxious to be rid of me?' Carlos asked.

'Anxious to get to work,' Marty retorted, although her habit of getting to work an hour or two early had only begun with Natalie's admission. Since Emmaline's birth, she'd been coming to work earlier and earlier, checking the baby first, then tackling paperwork, so she could free up small pockets of time later in the day to spend with the newborn infant.

'Not up to the NICU?' Carlos said, as Marty stood up and moved towards the sink with her coffee mug.

Marty spun towards him.

'What's that supposed to mean?'

'Exactly what I said! If you were not in the habit of visiting Emmaline before you started work each morning, I have seriously misjudged you.'

'And is that good or bad—this misjudgement thing?'

He held up his hands as she had earlier.

'It is neither. I have spoken clumsily. I am trying to say that I appreciate what you have done, and realise you have grown attached to the baby. I have nothing against you continuing to visit her. In fact, I would appreciate it.'

'Why?' Marty demanded. 'Because you have no intention of providing involvement yourself? Because working here is more important to you than getting to know your own baby? A few dozen scalpels, some old autoclave machines and a clutch of crutches for some people in Sudan are more important than your own flesh and blood?'

She took a deep breath, hoping it might calm her down, then added, 'You're right, I have been coming early and, yes, my first visit was usually to either the ICU or latterly the NICU, but the baby's father is here now, so she doesn't need me.'

'You called her "the baby",' Carlos said, the accusation in his voice mirrored in his eyes. 'So, having provided her with a bond, you'll now drop her—even drop the name you gave her? Well, I won't. I'll call her Emmaline and tell the nurses and doctors to do the same, and your friends will use the name and you will be the loser.'

He stood up and followed her path, carrying his cup to the sink.

'But Emmaline will also lose,' he continued. 'She will miss your company, your touch, your voice, and maybe have a setback—develop one of the complications so prevalent in low birth weight babies.'

He put down his cup and stood looking down at her.

'Is this fair to Emmaline? You may not like me, Martina Cox, but would you jeopardise that baby's health because of personal antagonism?'

It was a great exit line, Marty had to admit. She was still staring at the empty doorway minutes later. All she'd wanted to do was give him a clear field to get to know his child, and the wretch had twisted things around so she was the bad guy in this scenario.

Could Emmaline suffer a setback if she no longer visited the NICU? Right on cue, her mind conveniently produced a list of all the things that could beset such infants—hypoglycaemia, pulmonary insufficiency, apnoea and bradycardia—not to mention SIDS.

She'd have to work out a programme so she could visit Emmaline at unexpected times when Carlos was unlikely to be there, and though this would eventually make it harder for her to separate from Emmaline, at least she'd be sending home a well and contented infant.

She'd worry about her own contentment at a later date.

* * *

This would have worked if Carlos hadn't also chosen one of Marty's unexpected times to visit his daughter. Or maybe someone had contacted him to tell him it was feeding time, for he was holding Emmaline in his arms, peering down into her crinkled face, a look of bemusement on his usually impassive features.

Marty backed down the corridor, right into Sophie, who was heading for the unit.

'He looks as if he's holding an unexploded bomb,' Sophie remarked, nodding towards the tall man with the little pink bundle clutched gingerly to his chest.

'I think he might see her in those terms,' Marty replied. 'He feels she's already wreaked havoc in his life, he's just not sure when the next upheaval will take place.'

'Right about now,' Sophie predicted as a nurse approached with a feeding bottle. But although she proffered it to Carlos, he shook his head, handing back the baby with the tense arms of a man who was indeed holding a bomb.

'That's no way to bond with her,' Marty snorted, and was about to stride into the room and tell him so, but Sophie held her back.

'He has to do it in his own way and in his own time, Marty,' Sophie reminded her friend. 'You can't force someone to love their child. Love's organic—it needs time and nurturing in order to grow.'

Sophie spoke with the conviction of a woman deeply in love and Marty forbore to point out it had taken Gib and his new bride all of three weeks to decide they were made for each other, all of six weeks before they'd married.

But Sophie's words were comforting in a very different way, confirming Marty's belief that what she was feeling towards Carlos was a purely physical reaction and nothing whatsoever to do with love.

'I'd better go,' she said to Sophie, as Carlos moved towards the public exit from the NICU.

'You won't stay and feed her?'

Marty felt the ache in her chest that could only be alleviated by cuddling that small bundle in her arms, but the nurse would cuddle Emmaline and talk to her as she fed her and what was that, if not human interaction? It was during the time between feeds and changing that Emmaline needed company…

'I've got to wean myself away from her,' Marty explained, and Sophie, understanding, gave her a hug.

But avoiding Carlos was less easy. She had barely finished a planned Caesarean delivery of triplets when she was called to A and E—an ambulance bringing in a teenager with severe abdominal pain and vaginal bleeding.

Marty beat the ambulance, but not by much, and wasn't surprised to find Carlos by her side as the attendants wheeled the young woman, looking childlike in her green and white checked school uniform, into the trauma room.

'Regan Collins, fifteen, BP 120 over 65, pulse 90 and firm, temp 99.3, severe cramps and bleeding,' the ambo recited as he handed over the paperwork. 'We have her on fluid replacement but haven't done anything for the pain.'

'Because she could be pregnant,' Marty murmured under her breath to Carlos.

She stepped forward and introduced herself to Regan, who looked as if she needed a hug more than medication.

'You'll be OK,' Marty reassured her instead. 'We'll take a look at you and see what's what.'

The girl grasped her hand and squeezed it tightly, fever-bright eyes looking pleadingly into Marty's.

'You won't tell Mum,' she begged, and Marty's stomach tightened. She hated these situations—hated being the one who had to break her patient's confidence.

'You're a minor, Regan, and you were at school when this happened. The school will already have contacted someone in your family.'

'But I could just be sick—she needn't know what it is,' the girl said desperately, still clinging to Marty as if she held the promise of salvation.

'Well, I can't tell your mother what it is if I don't know,' she told Regan. 'So how about I examine you and we take it from there?'

'Mum can't know,' Regan wailed, then burst into noisy sobs.

Now Marty did hug her, gathering the girl's upper body in her arms and holding her close, making soothing noises as she patted Regan's back.

She used her free hand to smooth dark strands of hair back from the girl's face, while an errant thought flashed through her mind. Would Emmaline's hair stay black?

It was none of Marty's business.

'Hush now,' she said to Regan, when the storm of tears appeared to be subsiding. 'We'll sort it out.'

But Regan's head moved against her chest, denying this as an option, her drama-filled adolescent mind certain this was the end of life as she had known it.

'You can't, nobody can,' Regan cried, confirming Marty's thoughts, but the teenager allowed herself to be lowered back on the trolley so Marty could examine her, questioning her gently all the time.

When did she last have a period? Were they regular? Did she have a boyfriend? Was she having regular sex? Using protection?

Beside her, Marty could feel Carlos all but squirming— it was obvious why he hadn't become an O and G specialist! But when he murmured, 'I could never ask Sudanese women these questions,' she understood.

'Maybe a female nurse could,' she suggested, as she completed a gentle internal examination of the patient.

'It's all Rosemary's fault!'

Marty looked across at Carlos and smiled but he was looking slightly ill and so anxious Marty felt she should be reassuring him as well. He obviously didn't know that once teenagers starting blaming someone else, they were back in control.

'Why?' Marty said, and Regan started crying again.

But this time Marty continued about her business, asking Carlos to take some blood to go to the lab. 'We'll do beta HCG as well as the usual tests, and blood typing in case we need to operate,' she told him, knowing he'd know enough to realise the test for human chorionic gonadotropin would tell them if Regan was pregnant.

Or had been!

Palpating Regan's stomach, Marty found it to be soft, with no discernible lumps or masses, although Regan moaned with pain when Marty pressed on the uterus.

'We'll do an ultrasound now.'

'Rosemary said she knew how to get rid of a baby.'

Images of olden times—of back-yard abortions and quack remedies to bring on a miscarriage—flashed through Marty's head while her chest tightened with anxiety for the young woman—barely out of childhood—and the damage she might have done to herself.

But when she said, 'How was that?' her voice was gentle and contained, and Regan, taking heart apparently from Marty's tone, admitted to exactly what Marty had been dreading.

'With a knitting needle.' The words were little more than a breath of sound but the thought of the damage Regan might have done herself made Marty shudder. Although in early pregnancy, with the foetus so tiny, it was unlikely any amount of poking would have caused the miscarriage.

Regan began to cry again, but this time defensively.

'I had to do something! My mum would have killed me.'

'Instead of which you could have killed yourself if you'd got septicaemia or bled to death before someone realised you were in trouble,' Marty told her.

She wanted to say more—to wag her finger at the girl and yell a little. Say things like, 'Surely you've heard of safe sex? Surely by your age you know something about birth control. The pill?' but angry though she was about what she felt was the stupidity of teenagers, she knew now wasn't the time for a lecture. Later on she'd have to counsel the girl on just these things, but if Regan was angry and resentful towards her, she wouldn't listen.

The ultrasound revealed early pregnancy, now interrupted by this episode of blood loss.

'I need to take you into Theatre for a small operation to have a look in there and clean things up. We call it a D and C, dilatation—opening up your cervix—and curettage, scraping around your uterine walls.'

'That's gross!' Regan protested, then she brightened. 'But it'll get rid of the baby.'

'We're not doing it to "get rid of the baby", as you so bluntly put it,' Marty retorted. She was finding it more and more difficult to maintain sympathy for this self-focussed young woman. 'We're doing it to minimise the risk of infection and, far from being gross, it could well save your life.'

Regan must have picked up on Marty's mood, for a tear slipped from one eye and slid down her cheek.

'I've been stupid, haven't I?' she quavered.

'Very!' Marty agreed, but she gave the girl a warm hug. 'And although in the end things will be OK again, they're going to get worse right about now because we need your mother's permission to do the op.'

Carlos waited for the teenager's reaction, sure there'd be more histrionics. The more he'd seen of this particular patient, the more sure he'd become that he'd leave any O and G work, particularly with teenage patients, to whatever other medical or nursing staff he could beg or bribe to take over.

But the girl surprised him by accepting that her mother would have to know, although she looked pale, and so young Carlos felt his heart ache with sympathy for her. Then he thought of another girl—even younger—a baby girl high above them in the hospital.

He'd been beginning to think that, with sufficient help, he might be able to bring up a child, but no way would he be able to handle this kind of thing. Was it because she was a woman that Marty seemed a natural at it? Or was it her training that she'd been firm when she needed to be firm, while her underlying compassion came through in even her sternest words?

A nurse came in to tell Marty Regan's mother was here, and Marty nodded, then told the nurse with them to contact

Theatre to make arrangements for the minor op and for an anaesthetist to meet them there. She turned to Carlos.

'Will you go with Regan and the nurse to Theatre?'

This was colleague-to-colleague conversation, so why did he notice her eyes as they met his when she asked her question? And notice how fine her skin was—smooth, lightly tanned and unblemished except for a small freckle just above her lip on the left hand side?

In days gone by, women with such a mark would have darkened it to make a beauty spot, drawing their admirers' attention to the full lips beneath it.

'Carlos?'

Had he not answered her?

Had the sleepless night confused his mind to the extent he was distracted by a freckle?

'Of course,' he said, and saw a slight smile flash across Marty's face.

She suspected he was thinking of Emmaline—which he had been earlier.

'Keep Regan here a few minutes while I talk to her mother,' Marty suggested, as another nurse and an orderly came into the small trauma room.

Carlos moved to stand beside the girl while the nurse attached the drip to the small stand on the trolley and readied the patient for her move. Then Marty returned with an anxious, harried-looking woman, who rushed towards her daughter, caught her in her arms, and scolded her and hugged her all at once.

'Stupid, stupid girl! You know we can talk about anything, yet you didn't tell me. Honestly, Regan, sometimes I wonder if all your brains are in your toes. But you'll be all right, pet. The doctor will fix you up and everything will be fine, but I tell you, if you ever, ever pull a stunt like this again, I will personally kill you then cut you into tiny pieces and feed them to the dog!'

'Oh, Mum!' Regan sobbed into her mother's shoulder. 'I was so scared.'

'Of course you were,' her mother whispered brokenly, crying now as much as her daughter. 'All the silly stuff I told you about my getting pregnant too early and the struggle I had to keep you. Of course you didn't want to tell me.'

Carlos watched and listened with a sense of wonder and discovery, as if he'd sailed into foreign seas—or landed on a planet called 'Women'—and was learning firsthand just how different this world was. For these two were angry and upset yet obviously deeply loving towards each other in spite of the other emotions—the mother accepting, concerned, forgiving and nurturing all at once.

He could never handle that role for Emmaline…

It was obviously something only women could do…

He glanced towards Marty, who'd stood back and watched the reunion with that small shy smile on her face.

She already loved his baby…

'Moving time, people,' she said briskly. 'Ms Collins, you can come with us up to the next floor. There's a waiting room there where you can get tea or coffee. Do you have to let anyone know you're here?'

The woman shook her head, gave her daughter one last pat, then stood back so the professionals could do their job.

'She obviously loves her daughter very much,' Carlos murmured to Marty as they fell in a small distance behind the procession. 'So why was Regan so concerned?'

This time Marty's smile was just for him.

'It's complicated,' she said.

'That I had realised,' he assured her. 'But how? Why?'

'It's a lot to do with expectations,' Marty explained. 'For some reason they seem to grow exponentially with love. Because these two are very close, Regan feels far worse about disappointing her mother than she would if perhaps she had a less involved and caring mother. Her mother has probably always told her she can talk about anything with her, and Regan believes that, but she also feels that her mother would be disappointed in her if she found out Regan wanted to have sex with her boyfriend, so to avoid hurting her mother she didn't tell her.'

She smiled again, this time less shyly, and added, 'That probably doesn't make a jot of sense to you but, believe me, in the spider's web of mother-daughter relationships, it's near to normal.'

They'd reached the theatre and Marty was once again all business.

'I'd have suggested you do it for practice,' she said to Carlos, 'but given how the haemorrhage happened, I'd better see what's happening in there. If we leave a bit of tissue, she could end up with infection, and if there's damage to the uterine wall, I'll need to fix it.'

More than happy to be left on the sidelines, Carlos moved to stand beside the anaesthetist, who was questioning Regan about her health and explaining what she was about to do, inserting a mild sedative into the drip, attaching an oxygen mask, talking quietly and reassuringly as she worked.

Female anaesthetist, female surgeon—a woman's world again. Was he more aware of it because in Sudan he'd seen less of the women? Their husbands brought the children for attention, or brought their wives and explained their conditions, wary about letting a man touch—or even look at in some cases—their women.

CHAPTER THREE

'WAS the pregnancy compromised?' Carlos asked Marty, when Regan was in Recovery and Marty was completing her write-up of the operation.

She turned to study him for a moment, not answering— a questioning look in her eyes.

'And you're asking because?'

He shrugged his shoulders.

'Curiosity?'

She half smiled, but still didn't answer him, asking instead, 'Would you have seen it that way?'

He thought about it, considering the teenager's distress, the bond between mother and daughter, Regan's age and the complication a child could bring to her young life.

'I might have,' he said cautiously.

Then Marty let him off the hook.

'Yes, it was, although I'm pretty sure it was a spontaneous abortion and nothing to do with knitting needles. The pain she was feeling was definitely from the cramping of inevitable abortion—rupture of the membranes and cervical dilatation. I didn't answer you outright because I wanted you to consider the kind of issues you'll be dealing with once you venture into the world of O and G. And to have a taste of the decisions you might be called upon to make.'

She signed off on the operating notes with a flourish, pulled off her cap and ran her hand through hair so damp bits of it stuck up every which way.

'Would you have time for a coffee?' he asked.

'You have questions?'

He nodded, although he'd mentioned coffee more because he didn't want to be parted from her just yet. No doubt because she was the person he knew best in this foreign city.

Maybe.

'It's always coffee time for me,' she said.

An unexpected warmth that she had agreed to have coffee with him washed through him.

'I do have questions,' he said, following her into a small changing room where she shed her scrub suit, grabbed a clean one and pulled it on, bunching it around her waist and tying it with a head scarf to keep it all in place, as unaware of her appearance as a man would be.

Was that a sexist thought?

He suspected it was, but he was also interested to note that his body didn't see her as a man. For some reason it saw beneath the bunched-up suit to the womanly curves beneath.

No doubt because it was a long time since he'd had a relationship with a woman...

And remember where that led, his brain put in!

'My office is just through here—you're on the O and G floor—this theatre is for minor procedures or Caesars and is close to the delivery suite. My coffee-machine isn't quite as state-of-the-art as Gib's but it makes a passable cup of coffee.'

She led the way, nodding to staff they met in the corridor

then opening a door and showing him into a small but comfortable office, with three armchairs grouped around a coffee-table and a desk, decorated with all but toppling towers of books and littered with papers, crammed into the far corner.

'I do know where everything is in that mess,' she said, waving her hand towards the desk. 'My secretary despairs of me, but I get the job done.'

She picked up the phone and spoke to someone Carlos presumed was the despairing secretary, then came over to sit down in one of the armchairs, indicating with her hand he do the same.

'You had questions?' she prompted.

About so many things, he'd have liked to have said, but knew they were things he couldn't ask.

'Anaesthetic. You did a general—is that usual?'

'As against an epidural or something local?'

He nodded.

'The dilatation part of a D and C is very painful, and a mild general anaesthetic is easier to administer and requires a less…skilled isn't the exact word…anaesthetist, but most medical graduates can handle a general anaesthetic at a pinch. After all, they're trained to do it and always did it before specialisation became the norm. But any of the anaesthetic registrars can do a general, whereas some might have to call in their team boss for an epidural. Besides, I believe young girls—they're hardly women—of Regan's age like that don't need to be even partially conscious when they're going through something like that.'

So it was for the girl, Carlos thought, although Marty had put that part last. Were her thoughts always for other people?

But he was here to learn things other than the nature of

this woman and he remembered the other thing that had struck him as different.

'You scraped rather than suctioned in the operation. Was there a reason?'

A slight frown teased at her eyebrows, as if she hadn't really expected him to ask medical questions.

So what had she expected?

'I would usually suction, but I was worried the bit of teenage folly, prodding around with a foreign object, might have damaged the uterine wall and if I'd suctioned I might have started new bleeding.'

'I understand, and now we get to the issues I suppose I want to ask about. If she, young Regan, had been raped, would you have terminated the pregnancy for her?'

Marty straightened in her chair.

'You're getting out of straight medicine here, and into all kinds of dicey ethical issues. Personally, I try to do what the patient wants, but after a rape the patient's in such a difficult mental state there's no telling for certain if what they want right then is what they might want long term, so every case is a different kind of judgement call— every case needs to be weighed and discussed and considered long and hard. The only rule seems to be that there are no rules.'

She watched his face, and as she did so, realised this wasn't a question about Regan but about issues he might have to deal with every day.

'It happens where you work?' she asked gently.

He sighed, then nodded.

'Too often,' he said, his voice deepening as if despair and compassion joined to weigh it down. 'And the cultural and social repercussions are sometimes worse than the medical ones. In many cases, the girl or woman will be scorned by her own people—left an outcast through no fault of her own—and in such a situation maybe a baby, no matter how conceived, might bring joy and perhaps even solace.'

'Something good coming out of evil?' Marty queried, and again he nodded, his dark eyes soft as if remembering a particular case.

A soft tap on the door interrupted them and Marty called, 'Come in.' Her secretary, Karen, entered with a tray.

'I brought you sandwiches as well, because heaven knows when you'll get another break. You know you've got a specialists' meeting this afternoon at two?'

Marty assured Karen she did remember, then introduced her to Carlos, watching the way the young woman's eyes lit up with interest as she eyed the good-looking Spaniard.

Considering the way her own body was behaving in his presence, Marty could understand, though perhaps if she could hook him up with a girlfriend for the time he was here, her body would calm down…

The idea didn't seem nearly as good as it should and she was pleased when Karen departed.

Marty handed him a cup of coffee, offered sugar and milk, sugared her own, then took a sandwich.

'Karen's right,' she said, hoping her casually conversational tone hid what was going on both in her head and beneath her skin. 'In this game, you should eat whenever an opportunity presents itself as you never know when another one will come along. There's something tacky about munching on a sandwich in a delivery room where a poor woman has been in labour for eight hours.'

He smiled and she ignored her own reaction, then watched the smile fade.

'Is it legal in this country to terminate a pregnancy?'

It was the last question she had expected. No wonder his smile had faded!

'It depends on the circumstances,' she said, 'and although there are laws for all Australia which the federal government has put in place, every state has different laws and statutes about it. Why do you ask?'

He didn't answer immediately, finishing a sandwich while his eyes took on a distant look.

Because he was against it on principle?

But surely not, when he'd asked about termination in rape cases.

'I am wondering why Natalie didn't terminate her pregnancy,' he finally replied. 'Why, when she had come back to Australia to be with her true love, would she have kept my child?'

'Child support?' Marty said, tossing a flippant answer to cover the discomfort she felt discussing his dead wife.

'Child support?' he echoed. 'What is this?'

'I was being facetious,' Marty told him. 'Under our laws a father has to take some responsibility for his child even if he never sees it. It's worked out on a percentage of the father's income, which in your case I imagine would be nil or close to it, but in some instances a woman may opt to continue with a pregnancy knowing she will get money from the father to help towards the cost of child-rearing.'

It seemed a simple enough explanation, but she'd lost him. She knew that because the look in his eyes had gone from distant to far, far away.

'Child support,' he said again, barely breathing the words. 'It was for money!'

'But you can't know that!' Marty protested, defending the dead woman only she seemed to care about. 'Natalie must have felt something for you to have married you!'

Carlos shook his head.

'A degree of attraction perhaps, but that was all, and I knew it. However, in my country, arranged marriages still happen, particularly among families like mine, so I didn't see her lack of love as a problem. But returning to Peter Richards, who, even in Natalie's biased estimation, was a conman and a—she said no-hoper. Do you understand the phrase?'

'Only too well,' Marty told him. 'One of my half-sisters is married to one. He's always about to get a brilliant job, or start a can't-lose money-making scheme, and my sister continues to work full time to support him and their two children.'

'So,' Carlos continued, oblivious to Marty's relatives, 'a no-hoper might sometimes need some money?'

'*Always* need some money might be more accurate.'

She'd spoken before she'd realised there'd been sadness in his words, and now saw the pain on his usually expressionless face.

'You think she continued with the pregnancy in order to get money from you?' she guessed, then wished she'd kept her mouth shut, for he'd dropped his head into his hands and was kneading his scalp with his long, thin fingers as if to erase thoughts too hard to handle.

Instinct took her to her feet and she stepped across to perch on the arm of his chair and touch him lightly on the shoulder.

'This is all supposition,' she said, thinking now of Emmaline—of how he would feel about his child if he continued to think Natalie had gone through with the pregnancy for financial reasons. Wouldn't he hate the child who was the result of that pregnancy? Somehow, Marty had to make it right.

'For all you know, Natalie might have had very special memories of the time the two of you spent together and wanted to keep her baby as a reminder of those times.'

He didn't reply, though he did lift his head and settle back in the chair, which left Marty feeling foolish—not to mention distinctly uncomfortable about being so close to him.

She eased off her perch, moving towards the table, picking up the plate of sandwiches and offering them to him.

He took a sandwich then tilted his head back so he could look up into her face, and a sliver of a smile moved his lips.

'You think so?'

'We don't know!' Marty said valiantly, still trying to make things right for Emmaline. 'And that being the case, mightn't you just as well think that way as considering something negative?'

Now he did smile, but it wasn't a particularly joyous expression, and it failed to produce an accompanying gleam of amusement in his eyes.

'How old are you? Late twenties? Early thirties? You must see the worst that men and women can do to their fellow humans, yet you're still naïve enough to seek out the best in people?'

'It's better to look for the good than the bad,' Marty retorted. 'What's the use of going around in a permanent state of depression because bad things happen in the world? Thanks to television, we get instant wars and images of people like those you work with, starving because of the deadly combination of drought and war. But even in Sudan there must be things that make you smile—that bring you tiny scraps of joy.'

He poured himself more coffee and sat back again to sip at it, studying her as if she was some new species suddenly appearing, full grown, in front of him.

Then she caught a real smile, one that glinted in his eyes and creased the skin at his temples.

'Tiny scraps of joy,' he repeated softly. 'I like that. I saw a sunset one day—one particularly horrific day—when the sun splashed these brilliant red and orange colours across the sky. They reflected light a shade of pink that softened the makeshift hovels in the camp and turned the desert sand a deep purple. Human shapes were like stark, black shadows and the entire scene could have been a painting by a master.'

He nodded, remembering, then said again, 'Tiny scraps of joy,' in a voice so soft Marty barely heard it.

He looked across at her.

'You see Emmaline that way, don't you? As a tiny scrap of joy?'

'Message from Recovery,' Karen said, poking her head around the door. 'Your patient's had a cup of tea and biscuits and they're ready to move her to a ward.'

'I'll go and see her,' Marty said, pleased the interruption had saved her from either revealing how she felt about Emmaline or telling a lie. She could save both options for another day—sure Carlos wasn't the kind of man who'd let a question go unanswered.

'You want to come along?' she said to him, but the look in his eyes, as well as the conceding nod of his head, told her she'd judged him correctly. A day of accounting would come!

Regan had been transferred to a single room and was lying back in bed, looking sleepy, her mother by her side.

Marty asked the 'How are you feeling?' questions while studying the report from Recovery.

'You're still on the drip to replace fluid you've lost, and I'd like you to stay in hospital overnight,' she explained to Regan and her mother. 'As well as the drip, you'll be taking a drug called methergine eight-hourly today and tomorrow, which will help stop the bleeding, and an antibiotic to protect you against infection.'

The teenager was drifting off to sleep and Marty left the room, but Regan's mother followed her.

'Will you talk to her before she leaves?'

Marty knew exactly what Ms Collins meant.

'I will,' Marty promised, 'although I'm sure you've already drummed into her all the rules of safe sex.'

Ms Collins smiled for the first time since Marty had met her.

'I have,' she admitted, 'and I really believed she understood.'

The smile slipped from her face as she sighed, and added, 'But, then, I really believed she'd talk to me about things like this—that she'd discuss having sex with that worthless twit she calls a boyfriend before going ahead and doing it! I mean, she's been going out with him for two years—'

'She had a boyfriend at thirteen?' This was from Carlos who was frowning at the woman, but before Ms Collins could answer, Marty spoke again.

'Perhaps your estimation of him stopped her mentioning it,' she said, and the woman nodded.

'But I didn't know she'd get serious about him when I called him a worthless twit,' she protested. 'And, anyway, he is! He's a no-hoper, always slagging off school, hanging around shopping centres—a total no-hoper!'

Marty cringed at the description but this wasn't about Natalie and her boyfriend, it was about Regan.

'But Regan obviously likes him,' Marty said.

Beside her Carlos was muttering the word 'thirteen' under his breath, while Ms Collins was looking more and more distressed.

'She goes out with him because all her friends have boyfriends. It's peer pressure, nothing more than that.'

Carlos now took to muttering 'peer pressure' and Marty took Ms Collins by the arm and led her to the small visitors' room which was thankfully empty. She threw a glare at Carlos as she went, but he couldn't have been able to translate Australian glares for he followed them, although the muttering seemed to have stopped.

But once seated, Ms Collins broke down, weeping, blaming herself for what had happened, for not being a good enough mother, sobbing out how hard it was for a single parent to bring up a child.

'And just when you think you're doing all right—she's happy at school, and getting good grades—something like this happens.'

'It happens to kids who have two parents just as often,' Marty reminded her. 'And it isn't a reflection on the parents, or the girl's upbringing, or anything else. What you have to do is work out how you go forward from here. Regan's surgery wasn't life-threatening, but it will take a lot out of her. She's going to need all your love and support, not just while she convalesces but as she goes forward in her life. The two of you are going to have to sit down and work out some new ground rules, but you have to remember that teenagers are naturally secretive. They're convinced that what they're going through with puberty, romance, sex and so on is all new—that it's never happened to anyone else before—so naturally they can't be shocking Mum or Dad by talking about it.'

Marty was sitting on a couch, her arm around Ms Collins's shoulders, most of her attention on the distressed woman. But she glanced up as she finished talking, and saw Carlos looking at her, a wide-eyed expression of horror on his face.

She trailed back in her mind, trying to work out what she could have said to make him look like that, but it all seemed to have been very ordinary talk.

A page from Karen reminding her of her meeting meant she had to excuse herself before she could puzzle out Carlos's behaviour or finish reassuring Ms Collins, and though Carlos followed her out of the room, it was to excuse himself, saying he should return to A and E to do some of the work for which he was being employed.

'But later,' he said to her, 'in order to finish our discussion, would you have dinner with me?'

Marty was so stunned by the request she said yes before she'd had time to think it through.

Wasn't she already spending too much time with this man who made her feel things she didn't want to feel?

'I shall see you later, then,' he was saying. 'When do you finish work?'

Unable to back out of the dinner arrangement—unless, fortuitously for once, someone went into labour!—she agreed to meet him in the foyer after work. They'd walk home together and make the arrangements then.

Still worrying about the implications of all he'd seen and heard—and by immediately seeing Emmaline in the young Regan—Carlos detoured via the NICU before returning to A and E. He was standing by his daughter's cot, staring down at the little mortal, wondering why sleep was such an effort for her, when Sophie came to join him.

'I can't do this,' he said, saying out loud the thoughts he'd barely acknowledged to himself.

'Watch her sleep? Care for her?' Sophie hazarded.

'Go through her puberty!'

Sophie laughed.

'Haven't you heard of taking things one day at a time?' she teased. 'Yesterday you didn't know you had a daughter and now you're worrying about puberty?'

He stared at her, unable to believe she didn't understand.

'Of course I am,' he snapped, and walked away.

Marty would have understood!

But at nine o'clock that evening, he wasn't so sure. They were in Marty's apartment, in a spacious living area with glass walls that looked out towards the river.

It had been her choice of a place to eat as she had a patient in labour and might have to return to the hospital at any time.

'And it's easier to leave a half-eaten meal on the table at home than it is to rush out of a restaurant,' she'd explained, although she had agreed to order something in and allow him to pay for it rather than fix them both a meal herself.

Now, the meal having been eaten without any interruption, they were sitting in her deep leather armchairs, looking out at the river and sipping coffee—his with a drop of a mocha liqueur she'd wanted him to taste.

Fortified by a glass of a good red wine with dinner, and now the liqueur, he was ready to discuss the issues burning in his mind—and in his gut!

'This morning, Marty,' he began, less confident of her

understanding now than he had been in the NICU, 'what happened with that young girl—it struck home to me how ridiculous it is for me to even consider raising Emmaline. I can arrange a nurse for her while she is young, of course, but it is a parent's duty to speak of puberty and sexual behaviour. That would be impossible—'

'Nonsense,' Marty told him, lifting her coffee-cup and waving it towards him to emphasise her point. 'You're a doctor, you know what happens and young people appreciate facts.'

'That isn't what I meant,' he said. 'It isn't the practical that worries me. It is the emotional side of raising a daughter. I tried to tell Sophie about it but she laughed. She says I am thinking too far ahead, but if a father can't think ahead, who can?'

'Thinking ahead is good,' Marty told him although she wasn't sure where this conversation was going and didn't like any of the possible directions *she* could see ahead.

'Thinking ahead is disastrous!' he contradicted. 'It is terrifyingly obvious to me that, even apart from my present occupation, I am totally unfit to bring up a daughter. I tell you, Marty, when I saw that young Regan earlier today my mind went immediately to monasteries and I wondered at what age I could have Emmaline locked up in one, not to be released until she was twenty-one and a suitable marriage had been arranged for her. I have money, I could pay, and although there are fewer monasteries these days than in my forefathers' times, I am sure all of them are in need of funds.'

He sounded so serious Marty knew she shouldn't laugh, but she couldn't help it, rocking back in the chair and letting her delight at the picture he'd painted ripple out of her.

'It is no laughing matter,' he said sternly. 'Should she

come to me at, what, fifteen I think you said to tell me she was pregnant, I tell you I would have to kill the boy responsible. I can feel this in my heart, that just so would I react.'

His English, which was usually so good she barely noticed it apart from the accent, was growing muddled with his anger, and it added, as far as Marty was concerned, to the humour of the situation. She laughed again, although Carlos was now glaring at her, unable to see anything amusing in the teenage-Emmaline scenario.

She eased her mirth and pointed out that the teenage Emmaline wasn't the immediate problem.

'I know that!' Carlos snapped at her. He'd hoped for a serious discussion, not all this hilarity. 'But it is a foolish man who rushes into something without considering the long-term consequences.'

'Isn't it just!' she said, smirking at him now, reminding him of just how foolishly he'd rushed into at least one particular something without thought for any consequences.

His anger rose and found a focus.

'You think because you have the cool blood of your English ancestry in your veins and don't understand the heat of passion,' he growled at her, 'that you can take the high moral ground. But if I fired that blood, Marty Cox— if we shared a kiss that seared into your very soul and made you ache with wanting—would you think ahead to the consequences of conception, far enough ahead to fear your son or daughter's teenage years?'

He stood up and moved towards her, drawn by his mental image of just such a kiss and by his body's response to thinking about it.

'Could I fire you with a kiss? Do you believe I could do it?'

He was standing above her, his body throbbing, taunted by the languorous look in her heavy-lidded eyes.

'You'd hardly want to,' she said, and although she spoke lightly, he guessed she, too, was trapped by a sudden shift in the atmosphere in the room. 'I mean, look at me, your archetypal plain Jane! I'm jeans and T-shirt, not high fashion—short and dumpy, not slim and willowy.'

'You're a woman, and I'm a man,' he said, determined to prove his point, although somewhere deep inside he was distressed she should make light of her appearance. 'Sometimes that is all it takes.'

He leaned towards her, looking deep into eyes that had opened so wide a man could drown in them.

He's teasing you, Marty reminded herself, though her body was so taut she wondered if the slightest movement might shatter it. Taunting you because you had the hide to remind him of the consequences of his hot-blooded marriage.

But when he raised his eyebrows and looked down at her, she felt a shiver of pure anticipation, as if the kiss was already happening, his lips already pressed to hers, their tongues clashing in a dance that knew no language barriers.

He took her hand and drew her to her feet, not forcing her but allowing no resistance, then made the kiss a reality, his lips claiming hers with an arrogance that took her breath away.

At least she thought it was his arrogance, but by this time things were a little muddled and, seeking clarification of something, though she wasn't certain what, she kissed him back.

Fire and honey, heat burning with such sweetness Carlos wanted to lose himself in the pure sensation of the kiss. Her lips had trembled at first, then firmed and grew demanding, so his invasion of her mouth became a dance for two. He ran his hands down her back, learning the shape of her, finally cupping that pert bottom that had taunted him as they'd walked. It was all about shape, and her shape fitted his as if made for him, while her mouth was obviously another perfect fit, made for his kisses.

Soft breasts pressed against his chest as he drew her closer, trying to absorb all of her through the medium of his challenging embrace. But the challenge was now his for this wasn't a deliberate tease to jolt her out of her complacency, but something that seemed like the joining of two souls.

Fanciful nonsense, he told himself, then two slim hands wound around his neck, and thought gave way to feeling, his body flooding with a need that was shocking in its intensity.

'My pager is going to buzz any minute.'

The practical words, whispered against his cheek as Marty paused to draw breath, reminded him again of how this had begun, so when she eased away from him, he let her go, watching as she dropped, flushed and tousled, into the chair.

Had she turned the tables on him deliberately?

Fired his body with an aching hunger, because he'd challenged her to feel the heat of passion?

She ran her fingers through her hair, then looked up at him and smiled.

'Well, did you prove your point, or have you forgotten what it was?'

How could she do that?

How could she switch off like that as if what had just happened between them had been nothing more than a casual embrace?

He glared at her, seeing the little freckle just above her

lip and wanting to run his tongue across it—kissing her slowly this time, feasting on her...

'I think we should get married,' he heard himself declare, and, had he given it even an instant's thought, might have predicted her response would be another peal of laughter.

'Well, that was a reasoned, rational, well-thought-out decision,' she teased, still chuckling enough to colour the words with a warmth he hadn't heard before—or couldn't remember hearing.

Had no one ever teased him before? he wondered, trying to think back.

Or had they just not done it with the compassion that seemed part and parcel of the woman to whom he'd just proposed?

'I don't think so,' she said, and he knew she was deliberately keeping it light so he could get out of this situation without embarrassment, but the more he thought about it, the better the insane idea that had come from nowhere now seemed. She wasn't attached to anyone already, she had bonded with Emmaline, she could handle young women going through puberty, and if one kiss was any indication, they'd be extremely well matched in bed.

Somewhere in the back of his mind, a warning bell sounded—something to do with the fact that just so had he got himself into this trouble. But Natalie had been an entirely different proposition. Natalie would never have taken on a baby, let alone stuck around long enough for that child to reach puberty.

And he'd fancied himself in love with Natalie...

Love, as his mother had often said to him, shouldn't come into such practical arrangements as marriage.

But before he could explain all this to Marty, her pager did buzz and she excused herself to have a wash before she left for the hospital.

CHAPTER FOUR

'How do you get to the hospital at night-time?'

Carlos was standing by Marty's front door when she emerged from the hallway that led to her bathrooms and bedrooms.

'I jog,' she told him, pointing to the running shoes she'd put on. 'I owned a car when I moved in, but I found by the time I got it out of the parking area here then found a parking space at the hospital, it was faster to walk. Or jog if it's night-time and I haven't had a run.'

'Is your city so safe you have no fear, running at night?'

He'd followed her out the door and was standing close to her as she waited for the lift. Close enough to remind her body of the kiss they'd shared, and the hot spill of desire deep within that had been its response.

'It is relatively safe, but I'm not stupid.'

She pulled her personal alarm out of her pocket.

'I carry this—it makes a terrible wailing noise when it goes off—and there are always people around to come to the rescue. I'm quite adept at self-defence as well, so I'm not putting myself at unnecessary risk.'

The lift had arrived and they'd moved into it, Marty

nodding at a couple from a floor above who were already inside.

Carlos took her small alarm and examined it, then handed it back, his fingers brushing against hers in the exchange.

Could so accidental a touch have caused a hitch in her breath? She glanced up at him and saw evidence of a similar reaction in his eyes, then he smiled and desire surged again, although she knew his smile was an 'I told you so' smile, reminding her that he could make her feel the passion of which he'd spoken—reminding her this was a game to him.

'I'll run with you,' he said, and she looked him up and down. Black polo shirt in a silky kind of material, black jeans and black shoes too shiny to be joggers.

'In that gear?'

'Why not?' He shrugged, nodding to the other couple as the lift stopped on the ground floor then holding his hand against the door while Marty exited.

She stopped arguing, walking briskly through the foyer then slowly increasing her pace from a fast walk to a jog over the first few hundred yards. He kept up easily and it didn't take her long to realise he could have sprinted ahead and left her in his dust. Except that on the smooth paths of South Bank there was no dust.

Why had he come?

Altruism in that he felt protective towards her?

Or was it to do with his ridiculous proposal?

Maybe he wanted to explain why such a momentously stupid thing had issued from his lips!

But by the time they reached the crossing outside the hospital and nothing had been said between them, she realised he'd been doing exactly what he'd said he'd do— he'd run with her.

'I'm fine now,' she told him, wiping perspiration off her forehead with her handkerchief and wondering if she'd run faster than usual or if this man's presence had caused her to sweat.

'Can I not come in?'

'To see the birth? It will depend on the family. Not everyone wants onlookers. When I have students, I've always notified the family ahead of time.'

She must have sounded anxious for he touched her lightly on the shoulder.

'Don't worry. I will go and visit Emmaline while you have your baby, then walk you home.'

The thought of walking home with him, in darkness lit only by soft lamps, with the warm night air and river breezes wafting around them, made her shiver.

'Carlos,' she said firmly, as she got into the lift to go up to the O and G floor and he followed her in, 'I am quite capable of getting myself home. If it is so late that few people will be walking in the park, I'll get a cab. I do it all the time.'

'I will wait for you,' he said, and for the first time she realised he had a very stubborn jaw. Up till then she'd only seen the clean lines and angles of his face, but that jutting jaw was definitely stubborn.

'You won't know when I'm ready to leave,' she argued, giving him a bit of her own stubborn.

'I will visit Emmaline then wait for you in the foyer,' he announced. 'I can sleep anywhere, any time, so I will doze in one of the chairs.'

As good as his word, he was waiting, dozing in the foyer, when she came through it, smiling to herself after the safe delivery of a lusty baby girl.

She slowed her forward motion to look at him—to try to understand what it was about this man that had caught her interest—then realised he wasn't sleeping at all. In fact, he must have seen her enter the foyer for his eyes, beneath their sleepy lids, were tracking her progress towards him.

'You were supposed to be dozing!' she reminded him, disturbed by how his sleepy gaze made her feel.

'And let you sneak past me?'

Humour gleamed in his eyes, and her heart somersaulted in panic.

Don't do that, she wanted to yell at him, but how could she explain why? How could she tell him that a gleam in his usually expressionless black eyes made her feel things she didn't want to feel?

'If I'd wanted to avoid you, there are a dozen other ways I could walk out of here,' she told him instead.

He stood up and stretched and it seemed to Marty that the movement sent pheromones flooding through the air, snaring her in the sexual equivalent of a fishing net.

Impossible!

She stalked towards the door, furious at herself for getting entangled in his admittedly powerful sensual appeal. He caught up with her in a couple of strides, took her elbow as they crossed the road then, although she tried—subtly—to draw away, kept hold of it.

Not quite as bad as holding hands, she decided, then rescinded the thought. Elbow holding was far worse than hand holding as it drew their two bodies together.

'If we take this path to the right, will it bring us out on the river?' he asked, steering her towards the right-hand path without waiting for her reply.

'Yes,' she said, rather lamely, then realised this particular path led through an area of the park that was thickly planted with tropical plants to give visitors a taste of what a rainforest looked and felt like.

Thickly planted, and at night dimly lit! Scented with the heavy exotic scent of ginger flowers—a virtual lovers' lane…

Her body on full alert for another kiss, she stiffened as they entered the area where the lush ferns and big-leafed figs formed a tunnel that blocked out the sky. But her companion behaved like a perfect gentleman—so much so that Marty emerged from the shadows to the brightly lit walk along the river with a contrary sense of frustration.

It was soon eased for there was little wind and the glassy surface of the river reflected the lights of city buildings on the far side and, closer, shone with yellow balls of light, mirroring the lights along the river path, turning the scene she knew so well into an unfamiliar fairyland.

'That is a walkway?' Carlos asked, pointing to the Goodwill Bridge, spanning the river and providing pedestrian access from the city to the parklands.

Marty was about to agree, even tell him its name, when a cry drew their attention. A splash followed so quickly afterwards there was no doubt. Someone had jumped, or fallen, from the bridge into the river.

Marty reached into her pocket for her mobile phone but Carlos had already taken action. Pulling off his shoes, he'd climbed the low balustrade of the river path and dived in. He was now swimming strongly towards the centre of the river, his wake the only ripples marring the smooth surface of the water.

Where was the jumper?

Had he or she worn some kind of weight that they hadn't

surfaced? Marty's eyes searched the inky surface of the water as she dialled triple O and explained the situation, then pressed against the balustrade to watch Carlos swim.

The scene brightened, and with a stab of horror she saw the lights of an approaching ferry as it rounded the bend in the river, coming upstream towards the bridge. She panicked. Could the driver see someone in the water in the ferry's path? Would it be possible for anyone on board to see a swimmer at night?

Propellers—couldn't they chop a person to small pieces?

Fear for Carlos gripped her heart. She waved her hands and shouted, gathering a small crowd of onlookers even at this late hour, explaining what had happened, so the others began to wave and point and shout as well.

The ferry slowed, and a searchlight appeared, the beam travelling slowly across the water until it picked out the sleek dark head of Carlos and another figure, struggling furiously in his arms.

No need for CPR was her first thought, because she'd been subconsciously revising the technique in her head as she'd watched Carlos swim.

But she'd barely begun to relax when shouts and curses from the ferry tightened her anxiety another notch.

'Let him drown,' she heard someone yell.

'Watch the knife!' came from someone else.

A knife?

A police car pulled up beside her, the flashing red and blue lights reflecting colour on the river, adding a strangely carnival atmosphere to the tense stand-off. Next came a paramedic on a small motor scooter, fluorescent yellow bands across his uniform shirt.

Someone on the ferry cheered, and the long double-hulled vessel began to move slowly towards its floating pontoon, the crowd on the riverbank following on foot, anxious to be there when it docked so they could find out what had been going on.

The police car nudged its way through the onlookers, the paramedic following close behind, but one policeman had remained with the crowd, questioning people about who had phoned the emergency number.

'I did,' Marty volunteered. 'I'm a doctor at the hospital. My colleague and I heard a cry from the bridge then he dived in and swam out to where we'd seen the splash.'

The policeman took her name then asked for Carlos's name and address, saying he'd need to speak to both of them either later that evening or the following day. Marty wanted to protest that she'd already told him all she'd seen but knew he was only doing his job and taking witness statements was part of that. The ferry had berthed and the policeman jogged ahead to join his colleague, who was already walking down the gangway to the floating pontoon.

Marty picked up Carlos's discarded shoes and followed more slowly, knowing she wouldn't be allowed on board, but knowing also that she'd have to see that Carlos was all right before she could go home. The police would keep him longer, possibly have a paramedic check him out, then drop him home, she was sure of that, but she had to see for herself.

Because she was anxious for Emmaline's father?

She tried out the excuse for size but it didn't fit. Carlos Quintero's welfare had become personal.

Not a happy thought for a person who'd thought herself immune to physical attraction.

'Can we go?'

The object of her uneasiness appeared beside her,

dressed in his own trousers that dripped water around his socked feet, and with a too-small but dry sweater pulled on over his chest.

'You've spoken to the police?' she asked, and received a nod in reply, but that was all as his hand, once again with a firm grip on her elbow, propelled her through the crowd of onlookers and along the path.

'Are you all right? Someone mentioned a knife.'

She looked for signs of injury on his face, hands and wrists, but could see nothing.

'I may have a scratch on my chest but I didn't want to get caught up with the paramedic who had to see to the young man first. I'm relying on my own personal physician to have some sticky plasters at her home, should it be needed to pull the edges of the cut together.'

The casual words brought Marty to a halt.

'You *are* hurt!' she accused. 'How stupid not to wait and be seen by the paramedic. Is it bad? Did you look at it?'

He hustled her forward again.

'It is not bad but I am tired. Could we keep moving?'

And it was this admission, spoken through clenched teeth, that made her realise he was holding her elbow for support, not to guide her along the path.

'Here, this is better,' she said, sliding one arm under his arm and around his back and tucking her shoulder into his armpit so she could provide better assistance. 'But don't think I'll stop nagging about not seeing the paramedic. That was stupid behaviour.'

'The young man was high on drugs or alcohol. He needed three men to pull him onto the ferry then keep him subdued. Getting help for him must be a greater priority than my scratch.'

'Scratch!' Marty muttered. 'You're probably nursing a gaping wound and losing blood so fast you'll pass out before I get you home, but being a man you won't admit to an injury—that's probably closer to the mark than how much attention your young man needed.'

He didn't answer, but they were close to her apartment now and she'd see how bad things were before long. In fact, once in the foyer of her building, she realised it must be bad, for her forest-green T-shirt was patched with darker stains that she guessed were blood.

Up in her apartment, she led him, protesting that he was dripping water from his trousers, through to the bathroom, where she sat him on a stool and eased off his sweater, then gasped when she saw the wound. It slashed down across three ribs above his heart, gaping pinkly at her, not bleeding much but deep enough for her to see rib-bone in one part.

'You should go up to A and E and get it properly stitched,' she said, sure the steri-strips she had in her first-aid kit wouldn't be enough to hold the edges together.

'Are you telling me you don't have a doctor's bag—don't have a needle and some suture materials in it?'

She had to smile, remembering her graduation and her mother's pride when, the ceremony finished, she'd presented her daughter with a fully stocked medical bag.

Marty had protested she wouldn't have need for one as she intended specialising and working in a hospital, but she'd definitely found it useful, particularly during her training when she'd often worked with GPs to improve her general medical skills. Even now she kept it stocked for times a midwife doing a home delivery might call her out.

'You're sure you wouldn't prefer the hospital?' she

asked, worried now that she'd be responsible for stitching this man's skin.

Touching this man's skin?

'Just get it done,' he growled, and, realising that the sooner it was stitched, the better, she went to get her bag, glad she had some saline and iodine with which to flush the wound before stitching it.

She found what she'd need—saline, a local anaesthetic, needle and silk thread—and set them on a tray on the washbasin.

He sat on a small stool while she worked in front of him, her fingers trembling nervously, not because she was unaccustomed to the task—she stitched after every operation—but because this was Carlos, and the skin on his chest was as tanned as the skin on his face, smoothly tanned and stretched over slabs of muscle without an ounce of body fat.

Sensually soft, his skin, distracting her as she depressed the plunger on the syringe, administering a deadening agent to the nerves around the edges of the wound. Seriously tanned, his skin, distracting her even more as she pulled the edges of the wound together, to the extent that she, who would usually chatter as she worked, was too dry-mouthed to attempt a conversation. Beneath her fingers she could feel his heart beating, strong, steady strokes, while her own heart fluttered like a captive bird in her chest.

Trapped by attraction?

'There, done,' she said thankfully, and turned around to delve again in her bag for a dressing to put over it and keep it watertight. But Carlos's hands caught her waist, stopping her from moving, and she was trapped between his legs, his face on a level with hers, his eyes suggesting things that made her hot all over.

'I need to cover it,' she managed, though her mouth was drier than ever.

'I wish to thank you,' he said, so formally she began to think she'd imagined the messages in his eyes. 'In many ways,' he added, and she shivered, knowing she hadn't been wrong.

'I have to find a dressing,' she mumbled desperately. 'And it's been a long and tiring day.'

Uh-oh, shouldn't have added the last bit—it was a virtual admission that she knew exactly what he wasn't saying.

She tried to back away but his hands, though clasping lightly, held her prisoner. Or was it the power of those dark eyes that made moving an impossibility?

'Carlos?' she whispered, his name a plea she didn't fully understand herself.

'Marty,' he replied, her name on his lips as soft as a caress.

He looked at her for a long silent moment, then said, 'We are two adults who are attracted to each other—can you deny that?'

She couldn't but she wasn't going to say so, remaining mute, the feel of his long fingers pressed against the flesh at her waist sending rivulets of desire tingling through her entire body.

'So can we not explore that attraction?' he persisted. 'Forget that foolish suggestion of mine, forget the future for a while and see what happens?'

She opened her mouth to remind him where just such an experiment had led him once before then closed it again, knowing his marriage to Natalie was nothing to do with what was happening between them, though thinking of

Natalie made her feel sad, for how could a man who had loved such a beautiful woman be attracted to such an ordinary person as herself.

Lust! He was a man, and maybe he hadn't been with a woman for a while. Men's sexual needs, she firmly believed, were stronger than women's, although she wasn't at all sure that had ever been scientifically proved.

'Have you finished thinking about it?' he asked, bringing her mind back from a tangent of how such an experiment could be conducted effectively.

'I suppose we could,' she answered him, but he must have heard reluctance in her voice for her let go of her waist, eased her backwards just enough to enable him to get to his feet.

'Don't overwhelm me with enthusiasm,' he said tightly, then he moved away. Marty wanted to run after him, then remembered she had to find a dressing.

She, and the dressing, caught up with him in the front entry, where he was picking up his shoes.

'Let me put this on,' she said, and he smiled at her.

'Are you brave enough to get so close again?' he mocked, and she glared at him.

'It *is* late, and it *has* been a long day!' she protested, as she peeled the backing off the dressing and prepared to press it against his skin.

His tanned, silken smooth skin …

'And those are the only reasons we won't share a bed tonight?'

'No,' she snapped, pushed beyond endurance but aiming the dressing at his chest and pressing it home as she spoke. 'I won't share a bed with you tonight because I don't do one-night stands. In fact, I don't do relationships, full stop. For me it's far easier, and means much less wear and tear on my emotions, not to get involved in the first place than to get involved and then go through the messiness of getting uninvolved.'

He dropped his shoes as if so shocked by her statement he could no longer keep hold of them.

'You have a reason? You were hurt? We are human beings, Marty. We're not meant to go through this life without any physical comfort and pleasure. We do not have to commit to each other. My earlier question might have frightened you but, believe me, there need be no—the saying is no strings attached? We could not have kissed as we did if there wasn't an attraction between us, so why do you fight it? Is it a principle with you—perhaps a religious belief?'

Marty looked at him and saw genuine puzzlement in his face.

'If I were a sighing person I would sigh,' she told him. 'No, it isn't a principle, it's just a decision I made some time ago.' She should have stopped there, but suddenly she wanted to explain a decision she'd made three years ago after a particularly disastrous relationship but had never successfully explained to anyone, not even her mother.

'I can't have children, you see, and in previous relationships, in the beginning, when I explained this, the man has always said that was OK. Their take on it was like yours— we're just having a relationship and not considering anything beyond that. In fact,' she muttered, 'I think initially they liked the fact there wouldn't have been any accidental pregnancies. But somewhere along the line things would change and I would refuse to marry them because it wouldn't be fair to them, and they get upset and hurt, then I get upset and hurt and the whole thing's just one great shemozzle. Honestly, it's just far easier to not get involved.'

Hadn't he been listening that he picked on the least important part of the entire recital?

'You can't have children? Marty, *querida*.'

He gathered her into his arms, the movement so unexpected she didn't evade them, then couldn't escape once she was held tightly against his chest. He pressed kisses on her hair.

'For you, of all people, to whom it is abundantly obvious children are so important. Were you ill? Was it cancer? *Dios!* How can you live with it and be so open and so brave?'

He rocked her against his body like a mother cradling a child, but when the kisses shifted from her hair, slid down her cheek and finally caught her lips, there was nothing childlike in the feelings rioting through Marty's body.

'It is one more reason for you to marry me, for I already have a child,' he murmured, then he lifted her into his arms and carried her into her bedroom.

She tried to protest—reminding him of his stitches—but he ignored her, setting her on the bed then bending and kissing her once more on the lips.

'I am going now. You are right—it has been a long day and when I make love to you, it will be when you are fresh and we can be together all night long.'

And with that, and a final kiss, he disappeared out of her bedroom door. She lay there so bamboozled she couldn't move a muscle. Her front door opened then she heard the click as it locked behind her departing visitor. She stared at the ceiling, wondering if all that had happened this evening had really happened, or if, like Alice in Wonderland, she'd fallen through a gap in life into a parallel universe.

And rather than a Mad Hatter she'd found a crazy Spaniard.

CHAPTER FIVE

CARLOS hitched a hip onto a square concrete planter outside Marty's apartment, certain she wouldn't have left before six-thirty.

He'd slept well in spite of the air-conditioning, no doubt as a result of his unexpected swim, and had woken up that morning with a determination to get things right between himself and Marty.

But waiting here, outside her door, he wasn't so certain. He rubbed at the patch on his chest, where the stitches tugged, and tried to work out why it mattered.

Because of Emmaline was the easy answer.

Marty was the ideal person to take charge of Emmaline.

A stab of pain and he pressed his hand against the stitches, certain it was them and not Marty's confession that had caused it.

'Your trousers are dry so presumably you didn't spend the night in that pot-plant.'

He turned to see her standing right behind him, a small, neat figure in what seemed, for her, to be almost a uniform—jeans and T-shirt. Today's jeans were pale blue denim faded almost to white, and they tucked around the curve of her backside in a way that made him want to cup his hands against the fabric and pull her close against his body.

'How's your chest?'

Was she looking flustered as she asked the question or had she put the events of the previous evening so far behind her she no longer remembered them?

'It is well, thank you.'

He could do formal as well as the next person—better than most, in fact, having been brought up in an extremely formal household.

'Good,' she said, then moved briskly away, leaving him to catch up if he wished to.

Or not!

He was tempted toward the second option. He would give up this pursuit of a woman who clearly didn't want to be pursued, phone his mother to explain about Emmaline, and ask her to fly out and take the baby back to Spain. Emmaline would fit right in with his sisters' children, all of whom lived in apartments in the family home, and the nursemaids they employed could care for Emmaline as well, with his mother overseeing her upbringing.

He'd visit, of course…

He reached this point in his eminently practical plan before he heard Marty's voice in his head, berating him for thinking that visiting was doing his duty as a father. Ahead of him, the curves of her bottom moved cheekily against the faded denim, reminding him of the option he'd been about to dismiss. He lengthened his strides and caught up with her.

But if he'd thought walking beside her was better than being distracted by walking behind her, he had to think again, for being close to her reminded him of how her

body had felt against his, and how her kisses had, so un-
expectedly, fired his blood.

'What kind of equipment and supplies are most needed
where you work?' she asked, and it took him a moment to
detach his mind from carnal thoughts and divert it back to
medical ones.

'We get good supplies of drugs and dressings from
various manufacturers who use their donations as a tax
write-off, but even something as common in your specialty
as a speculum can be hard to come by. Things disappear,
too, and it is hard to blame people who have so little for
taking something that might be useful to them.'

'A speculum could be useful to them?' she queried, her
eyes slanting in humorous delight towards him.

He refused to smile back because he'd managed to make
the switch to medical thoughts and wasn't going to be
enticed away from that path.

'It has a screw mechanism that someone might think
they could use in another application. Scalpel blades are
the most sought-after commodity, but so dangerous we are
particularly careful to keep track of them and to dispose of
those that can no longer be used by melting them down in
a small furnace donated for the purpose. Let the scaven-
gers have the lump of metal!'

She shook her head.

'It blows my mind, hearing of these things. It's something I've often thought I'd like to do, work overseas, in a
country where I might be needed, but...'

'But?'

No reply.

At least he knew it wasn't a man keeping her in Australia.
But comforting though that thought was, it wasn't

enough. He wanted to know the reason Marty had stayed here—in fact, he wanted to know a whole lot about this woman who walked by his side.

That she was a private person he already knew—and that he, possibly because of his relationship to Emmaline, had broken through part of the barrier she'd erected to hide behind, he also knew. Her confession about not being able to have children told him that much.

They reached the hospital and he watched her shoulders rise as she drew in a deep breath.

'I was going to go up and spend some time with Emmaline,' she said, 'but if you're planning on doing the same, I can always find some paperwork that needs my attention.'

'Why can't we both go?' Carlos asked, then wondered what he'd said that Marty turned to him, a look of absolute horror on her face.

Go with him to visit Emmaline? As if the two of them belonged together? As if they were her parents?

Marty was having a hard enough time getting her head straight as far as Carlos was concerned, without playing happy families with him and Emmaline.

He'd stopped walking and caught her elbow, turning her so she was facing him, obviously waiting for an answer.

Suggesting he was out of his mind occurred to her, but she went with a more reasoned, rational reply.

'Because!' she snapped, then tugged her elbow free, striding through the main foyer to the lifts where she pressed the 'up' button.

'Succinct but hardly explanatory,' he murmured, coming to stand far too close beside her, but in spite of the effect of his closeness, her mind registered just how good his English was that he'd know a word like 'succinct'.

'If you wish to visit Emmaline before you begin work, but without my presence, I can make myself useful in the A and E.'

Marty felt her stomach clench. It was a victory, but not sweet. She was being petty, and now she thought about it, might it not be easier for him to visit his daughter with someone else there to make it seem less awkward?

'No,' she muttered at him. 'Let's both go! But don't go thinking it means anything.'

He looked perplexed and she realised he'd never considered the images of family and togetherness that had put her in a spin. Manlike, he had simply thought the two of them could visit together.

They rode together up to the NICU floor and walked through into the big nursery, where the soft strains of one of Mozart's piano concertos filled the air with gentle melody. A nurse who was lifting the tiny girl from her crib smiled when she saw the pair of them approaching.

'Great timing. It's change and feed time. You'll note she's no longer hooked up to monitors, although there's a sensor on her mattress in case her breathing gets erratic.'

She handed the little bundle to Carlos and Marty watched as he cradled her in his big hands, peering down into her face as if trying to find some familiar feature.

'She sleeps with such concentration,' he said to Marty, turning his hands so she could see Emmaline's face. Then the eyes slowly opened and found a focus not on Marty's face but on Carlos's, and Marty heard him catch his breath as the deep blue eyes, so dark they were almost black, looked into his.

'She's awake but doesn't cry,' he said, a note of wonder in his voice. Marty wasn't going to spoil this moment for him, but the nurse had no such inhibitions.

'Very few premmie babies cry,' she said. 'It's something they start later when they learn how to make their needs known. If they're distressed, they might go pink, and sometimes you hear a thin wail, but generally they're very quiet.'

She led them to a table at the side of the room, where a lamp provided extra heat for babies being examined or changed. She handed Carlos a clean nappy and then a plastic bag already marked with Emmaline's name.

'What is this?' he queried.

'For the used nappy,' Marty told him. 'It will be weighed so her urine output can be measured and a drop of the urine tested to make sure she's not harbouring some dread disease.'

He shook his head as if in wonder, then watched as the nurse unwrapped his daughter from her blanket, removed the nappy, sponged the little body then stood aside.

'Your turn,' she said to Carlos, who looked at the object in his hand then at his tiny daughter, and shook his head again.

'Go for it!' Marty encouraged, watching with amusement as he gingerly set it down, then lifted the wee legs and settled it under the non-existent butt, before bringing the front part up and securing it in place with the plastic tabs.

Then she waited, smiling, for she knew from experience that if you picked up the baby without swaddling her first, the nappy would slide right off.

'I knew I'd be no good at this,' Carlos said in frustration as the nappy did exactly as Marty had predicted and dropped to the floor.

Both the nurse and Marty laughed while the nurse produced a second one and suggested he try again.

'That always happens,' Marty told him. 'When they're left unwrapped because of the monitor leads attached to their chests, you have to hold it in place when you lift them, but now Emmaline's off the monitors, you can swaddle her and keep it on that way.'

Carlos repeated his effort with the nappy, then watched as the nurse wrapped Emmaline so her legs were tucked up in much the same position she'd have been in while in the womb. Once satisfied she'd tucked in all the ends, the nurse lifted the little bundle and handed her to him once again.

'Feed time,' she said, and though he turned as if to pass the baby to Marty, she ducked backward out of passing range.

'Your turn,' she told him. 'There's a quiet room where you can do it in comfort. I'll lead the way.'

The nurse handed him a small bottle containing warm formula and he followed Marty to the quiet room and sank down into a comfortable armchair.

He cradled the baby against his chest and pressed the teat into her mouth, seeing how the little lips closed around it and hearing the welcome sound of sucking.

'She feeds well,' he said in wonder. 'So small but she knows she needs this food.'

'Either that or she's a greedy little minx and she'll be the size of a house before she's six.'

Marty smiled as she spoke, but the image of a small fat child with straight black hair had popped obligingly into Carlos's mind and he went into panic mode again.

'How do you know what is healthy eating and what is greed?' he demanded.

'I guess you just know,' Marty said. 'I really don't

believe she's greedy—she's just a very good feeder and, as far as I know, children regulate their own eating. As long as they're not fed heaps of junk food or are snacking all day on lollies or chips, most of them grow up healthy.'

But Carlos had only heard part of the conversation, Marty's words suddenly meaningless as his daughter's eyes opened again, finding then fixing on his face, and he felt a surge of possession so strong a shudder ran through his body.

How could he think of sending this child away to be brought up by strangers? Even with his mother there, it would not be enough. Visits home would be agony because instead of this recognition the little one seemed to feel toward him already, there'd be confusion as she tried to figure out who he was all over again. It would not be fair on her to have to grow up in such a way.

He looked at Marty, who was watching Emmaline feed with the same kind of concentration Emmaline was using on him. Marty was the answer. She loved the child, so why would she not want to be part of her upbringing? If Emmaline had a mother with her all the time, rather than aunts and nursemaids and a grandmother, then his returns and subsequent departures would be less traumatic for the child.

He would marry Marty!

The only other option appeared to be to give Emmaline to Marty to bring up—to bow out of Emmaline's life altogether.

His arms tightened subconsciously around the baby and he realised this wasn't an option after all. This was *his* child, looking so trustingly up into his face. How could he betray that trust?

'You can talk to her as she feeds.' Marty's words interrupted his thoughts. 'She won't get distracted and it's an opportunity for her to get to know your voice.'

Emmaline had turned as Marty spoke and Carlos felt a surge of pride that, tiny as she was, his daughter could recognise Marty's voice. But then the dark eyes swung back his way and this time it was satisfaction that flooded his body. She'd chosen him to look at, not Marty!

'She watches whoever is feeding her—most babies do!'

'Did you read my mind that you knew what I was thinking?' Carlos demanded, embarrassed to think he was so obvious.

'Not your mind,' Marty told him with a smile, 'but the smug look of satisfaction on your face. It all but yelled, *See, she likes me best*!'

Carlos frowned at her, but deep inside he felt a rightness that the three of them were sharing this time.

Should he say something?

'I heard you three were in here.'

Too late! He turned to see Gib standing just inside the door.

'Sophie and I were wondering, Marty, if you and Carlos would like to come to dinner tomorrow night. We're having a few of the staff around to celebrate the hospital's decision to expand our teams—we're taking on an extra graduate in the training programme. It won't be anything fancy—most probably a barbeque—and bring your togs if you'd like a swim.'

'Togs?'

'Swimming costume,' Marty translated for him, then turned to Gib. 'I'm off duty so you've got me. What time?'

'Around seven. You'll bring Carlos? We can take the opportunity to talk to folk in other specialties about his needs so they can all get busy hunting out stuff they don't use for him to take back to Sudan.'

Back to Sudan! The phrase echoed in Carlos's head as he stared down at the infant in his arms.

Bringing up Emmaline—being involved with her on a daily basis—was really an impossible dream. He had to be practical about this and think with his head and not his heart.

And he had to think about it right now, before his heart was engaged any further by this child…

'He seems to be in a fugue state right now, but if you're offering to publicise the plight of his patients, I'm sure he'll be willing to attend,' Marty was saying, and though Carlos knew she was talking about him, he couldn't join in, or even pretend amusement at her words. He stood up, holding Emmaline carefully, and carried her back into the nursery.

Marty was aware something had happened in the quiet room off the NICU, but just what, she wasn't sure. As Carlos had left the room, she'd answered a page from A and E, going down to the emergency room to find a woman travelling around Australia with her husband in a campervan about to give birth six weeks before she was due.

Sally Green was fully dilated, with severe, minute-apart contractions, making it impossible to use drugs to delay the birth. Before accompanying her up to a birthing suite, Marty asked one of the nurses to contact the NICU. She wanted a neonatal team on hand when she delivered this baby. Their care and expertise in stabilising premmie babies immediately after delivery had saved the life of innumerable infants and meant better outcomes for countless others.

By the time they reached the suite, the team was already there—Gib himself, a respiratory therapist, a neonatal nurse and—guess who? Carlos Quintero! As if watching him nurse and feed his daughter hadn't been enough for Marty to bear already that morning, she would now have him here during a delivery.

At least it should be straightforward, Marty thought as she introduced Gib's team to the expectant parents and explained why they were there.

But was it ever straightforward?

With an excited father causing more anxiety than the labouring woman, Marty let the baby's head ease gently out, holding it face down while a nurse ducked beneath her to wipe the mouth and nose and gently suction the mouth. But Marty's questing fingers had found a loop of cord and she warned Sally not to push until the loop could be passed over the baby's head so it wouldn't strangle the infant during the delivery.

But as Marty lifted one loop and eased it over the head, her fingers felt the second—the cord wasn't looped once but twice.

'Clamps,' she ordered, holding the head firmly so the next contraction couldn't push it further out. The small cord clamps slapped into her left hand. With one hand still holding the baby's head, she clamped the already freed loop of cord in two places, then cut between the clamps and unwound the loose end from around the infant's neck. 'We're OK now,' she told the father. Will Green had abandoned his wife and was leaning over Marty's shoulder as first one shoulder and then the other slid out into view.

'Now's when we hold on tight,' Marty said to him, 'because the rest might come in a rush. You want to do it? One hand under the head and body and the other ready to catch the buttocks and legs.'

Will stepped forward, then backed away.

'I might drop him,' he said, his voice quavering with apprehension. 'Or her!' he added, probably just in time as far as Sally was concerned.

The baby slid out easily, and Marty watched in satisfaction as the purple-blue body turned a healthy pink. She turned to Gib, a question in her eyes, and saw him nod. She wrapped the little infant in a cloth and passed him to his mother, where he nestled against her breast, nuzzling the softness, his lips moving as he sought a nipple.

'Maybe not as premmie as we thought,' Gib murmured, and Marty looked across at Will, who was examining his newborn son with a look of awe on his face, while tears dribbled unnoticed down his cheeks.

'How sure were you of the dates?' she asked, and he looked up at her and frowned as if he didn't understand her question.

'The baby's due date?' Marty clarified.

'Oh, when the baby was due? Well, we were never really sure. Someone said you worked it out from the time of my wife's last period—'

'But I've never been all that regular,' Sally put in. 'So we didn't really know.'

'Have you seen a doctor at all during the pregnancy?' Marty asked, and received puzzled expressions from both of them again.

'I had a cold when we were in Western Australia,' Sally said. 'I went to the doctor then because I didn't want to take anything that might upset the baby.'

Marty gave up. Hadn't women had babies this way for thousands upon thousands of years—doing what came naturally? In this case, it had all worked out well. The neonatal nurse had taken the baby to be weighed and tested, cleaned and dressed, and the weight alone was enough to have the team stand down.

'Weight, reflexes, cry and skin texture—see the peeling—they're all providing evidence that, if anything, this little chap was overdue,' Gib told her when she joined him at the table in the corner of the room. 'But as we're here, we'll do the normal newborn post-delivery procedures.'

He turned to Carlos.

'We routinely administer vitamin K intramuscularly to prevent haemorrhagic disorders and recommend a hepatitis B vaccination these days. I imagine in Sudan you'd need that and, if the mother is a carrier, then hep B immune globulin should also be administered at another site.'

'If the mother happens to have her baby at the hospital or where medical help is available,' Carlos told him. 'Actually, hepatitis is a problem over a lot of Africa. Before I left Sudan this time I was asked if I'd be willing to go to Botswana to help with a UN programme they hope will eventually eradicate it.'

Sudan! Botswana! Marty heard the names and felt a tug of longing to see these far-away places and to work with the people.

But there was Mum! Although she knew her mother would be only too willing to accompany Marty to such places, the problem of keeping both of them on the small stipend most of the aid organisations could afford to pay their workers had always held Marty back.

That and the fact that her mother would refuse to be kept! She'd worked all her life and, as she often informed her daughter, had no intention of stopping now.

Marty showed her patient how to massage her own

abdomen to help expel the placenta, and once that was delivered and examined to make sure it was complete and had no anomalies, she left the couple to the ministrations of the nursing staff. Carlos had accompanied Gib and his team out of the suite, and for the rest of the day she was, thankfully, not involved in any sudden admissions.

In fact, by the time she was due to leave the hospital, the day had been so predictable, even boring, that she'd begun to wonder if O and G had always been like that. But she knew it wasn't the lack of emergency work that had seemed to dull her day but the absence of the person working in A and E.

She dismissed the thought, considering instead what she might wear to the barbeque, then laughed at this new thought which was, on consideration, the same as the previous one. It was a barbeque and she'd wear jeans and a T-shirt—what she always wore wherever she went...

To take her mind off clothes, barbeques and a person working in A and E, she phoned her mother before leaving work, intending to invite herself to dinner.

'Oh, no, Marty, I'm sorry but it's the fourth Friday.'

'Is that like the Ides of March?' Marty asked and her mother laughed.

'No, it's Scottish country dancing night. Second and fourth Friday—I thought you knew.'

'I did know you'd been to classes, Mum, but obviously hadn't picked up on the regularity of it. Are you enjoying it?'

'Love it!' her mother said, so wholeheartedly Marty felt warm all over. Had she ever heard her mother talk about something with such enthusiastic delight? Well, yes, but in the past her delight had usually been for Marty's exploits or triumphs.

'That's great!' Marty told her, then chatted for a while before wishing her mother luck in the dancing and hanging up. But as she did so, she felt an inexplicable sense of loss, as if the mother she had always known had somehow changed.

Had her voice sounded different?

Was there more to her enjoyment than just the dancing?

A man?

The thought was so bizarre Marty dismissed it immediately, then immediately after that paused to consider the possibility.

Her mother was an attractive woman in her early fifties, and just because, until now, she hadn't shown any interest in finding another partner, it didn't mean that, should a man have happened along, she might not have considered it.

Had a man happened along?

A dancing man?

A Scottish man?

'You're thirty years old and your mother is entitled to her own life!' Marty muttered to herself, then glanced cautiously around to make sure Carlos hadn't sneaked up on her to overhear her mutters.

Carlos! In spite of all her best efforts, and the distraction of her mother's happy voice, Marty's mind did keep whirling back to him.

Well, it would, of course. What with Emmaline, and his ridiculous proposal, and the kiss, of course she'd be thinking of him from time to time!

Thinking of him with a tingling of desire in her nipples and a flicker of heat spearing down her belly?

The jangling demand of the phone broke into her thoughts and she lifted the receiver, pleased to have a diversion.

'You are going home?'

Some diversion! Velvet accented tones sneaking into her ear. Images of the long, lean, suntanned man flashing through her mind.

'Eventually,' she said.

'You have work to do?'

The man was nothing if not persistent.

'No, but I thought I'd stop on the way—there's a great Chinese restaurant down by the river that a lot of the staff frequent, and I often eat there on my way home on a Friday night.'

Now why had she told him that? What she usually did on a Friday night was work, or work out at her gym, kicking the hell out of boxing bags to release the tension of the week.

'May I join you?'

It would be so easy to say no, Marty reminded herself, but somehow her lips wouldn't form the simple word.

'I suppose so,' she said instead, wondering if he understood the word 'grudgingly' and if he'd have heard it in her voice.

Apparently not, for he was cheerfully making arrangements to meet her in the foyer.

'I will be the person not sleeping this time,' he said, and she had to smile.

But before going to meet him, she went to the washroom, where she studied her reflection in the mirror that ran along the wall above the washbasins.

'Why?' she asked the face that looked back at her. A neat enough nose, lips that were more useful than decorative, eyes that always seemed a bit too big, especially when she was looking tired, and wispy, not quite blonde hair framing the unremarkable features.

'Because he needs a mother for Emmaline!'

She answered her own question and slumped against the washbasin, frightened by the fact that part of her considered this a reasonable proposition. She would get Emmaline and an occasional husband.

Or would she?

Would he keep coming back to someone like her?

He might, because of Emmaline...

She shook her head, wishing for just an instant she had long blonde tresses that would swish around her shoulders when she moved in just this way, then she laughed at herself for being ridiculous, and found laughing at herself was just as painful as having other people laughing at her...

Though the person who pushed through the door wouldn't laugh at her. They'd shared confidences in this washroom before today.

'Getting caught laughing at yourself in the washroom is better than getting caught crying, the way I was,' Sophie said, reminding Marty of the time she'd found Sophie in tears in the same place.

'I think my laughing was much the same as your crying,' Marty admitted, and Sophie touched her lightly on the shoulder.

'Carlos?'

Marty nodded.

'Well, you've certainly got taste,' Sophie teased. 'If I wasn't so besotted with my new husband, I'd have been attracted to him, too. Does he like you?'

'Did you see Natalie?'

Sophie nodded her head, but refused to be put off.

'So his wife was beautiful, but apparently the marriage

didn't last for all that. And you're not exactly dog-like in the looks department. You've got a great figure, lovely eyes, but you don't give yourself a chance because you have this tendency to pull on the first clothes you touch when you reach into your closet. So I'll repeat the question—does he like you?'

Marty studied her friend for a moment, then shrugged.

'He sees me as an answer to his problem of finding a mother for Emmaline,' she admitted.

Sophie, with a whispered 'Oh!' gave her a warm and comforting hug.

'At least you're predictable,' she grumped at Carlos as he stood up at her approach.

'Predictable?'

'Same chair,' she explained, waving her hand towards his chosen waiting place.

'Ah,' he said, staring down at her with an intense expression in his eyes. 'You have had a bad day.'

'Actually, I've had a very ordinary day,' she said, striding out of the hospital, though not losing him as he could easily keep up. 'Even boring, which is something I never thought my job could be.'

'No, I can't imagine anything in your life being boring,' he said.

'Which just shows how little you know about me,' she snapped. 'Even my mother has a better social life than me. And my clothes—jeans and T-shirts! When did that become a uniform? Boring? I could give lectures in boring. I could bore for Australia!'

'Your shops are open in the city this evening? Do they stay open at night?'

It was such a peculiar question, coming as it did out of the blue, Marty didn't answer for a moment. Then she realised it was his attempt to get her off her rant on boring and told him that they were open on Friday nights only, for late-night shopping.

'You need to shop?' she said, thinking he might prefer to go immediately rather than eating first. In which case she could go back to her boring flat and get really depressed about her boring life!

'No,' he said. '*We* need to shop. You have been very good with Emmaline. Gib has told me how you visited and played music and talked to her before she was born and I have been thinking how to say thank you. So we will shop. We will pretend you are my mistress and I am going to shower you with presents and you will try on clothes and I will sit and look at you and say whether or not we buy them, and we shall have a wonderful time.'

'That's the most ridiculous suggestion I have ever heard,' Marty protested. 'I don't want clothes—I don't need clothes—and as for your paying for them...'

She didn't mention the mistress thing, which had caused a quite ridiculous flutter of excitement in her chest.

'It will be fun,' he persuaded. 'Not boring at all.'

'But I don't want you to buy me clothes,' Marty told him, although she suspected she was missing the point. What she didn't want was *any* personal interaction with this man, particularly interaction that could conceivably come under the 'fun' label. But for all the notice he took, she might as well have been talking to the river—telling it to stop flowing to the sea.

'I refuse to be swayed,' he announced. 'We will walk over the jumper's bridge to your city and we will shop! And do not argue. If necessary, I shall throw you over my shoulder and carry you to the shops.'

He took hold of her elbow and steered her down the path that led to the pedestrian bridge. Marty was unsure how to counteract this determination—unsure also why the idea of being thrown over Carlos's shoulder and carried anywhere wasn't nearly as horrifying as it should have been.

'Do you have some kind of radar that draws you to the most expensive shops?' she demanded a little later, as Carlos steered her into a new boutique in a new arcade, with the clothes arrayed in bright beauty along the walls and a comfortable sofa set in the middle of the shop, seemingly for the express purpose of Carlos's sitting thereon while looking at her in fancy clothes.

Burning with embarrassment, but excited at the same time, she accompanied Carlos into the shop. He spoke to the woman who greeted them and to Marty's overwhelming relief told not the mistress story but the truth.

'We are colleagues,' he announced, 'and I owe her a great personal debt, so we will do a—do you call it a makeover? Her wardrobe currently consists of jeans and T-shirts so anything, you will agree, will be an improvement.'

Marty felt obliged to object to this statement but the saleswoman was so intrigued—or perhaps so fascinated by Carlos's dark good looks—that she ignored Marty's protest that her clothes were sensible and practical.

Instead, she escorted Carlos along the racks and shelves, pointing out this or that, glancing back at Marty from time to time, as if assessing her, discussing with him fabrics that Marty had never heard of.

She should never have come.

And now she was hungry, her stomach reminding her

how long it had been since lunch, but Carlos was listening to an explanation from the saleswoman and, much as Marty would have loved to walk out, there was a little bit of her that was not excited but certainly intrigued by the prospect of a transformation.

No way she'd turn into a swan, but she hadn't been an ugly duckling to begin with. Just short and ordinary— hardly swan material.

'Ellen is ordering us some sandwiches and wine,' Carlos announced, coming across to Marty while the woman went back to her desk to phone. 'And she thought you might wish to shower before you try on clothes, and will show you where to go and provide a robe.'

I should stop this right now, Marty thought, but she did feel rather sticky, and a shower seemed like a wonderful idea. She accompanied the woman down a passageway at the back of the shop, and into a bathroom that was luxurious in its appointments.

'I had it done especially,' Ellen explained. 'A lot of women choose clothes at all the wrong times of the day and because they don't feel fresh and excited, they don't like what they put on.'

'The things you learn,' Marty muttered, then thanked Ellen who was hanging a thick white towelling robe on a peg behind the door.

But once showered, Marty found her clothes had disappeared. And on the padded stool where she had left them were three sets of the prettiest underwear she had ever seen. Tiny red rosebuds were embroidered on pale green satin, the little knickers shaped like miniature boxer shorts, while the bra was as light as thistledown.

Three different sizes, and Ellen proved a good judge as

the middle set fitted perfectly. But as Marty looked at herself in the unaccustomed underwear, she wondered how often Carlos might have done this for other women, and a sick feeling in the pit of her stomach suggested she should stop the charade right now.

But how to do it was the problem. Take off the underwear, march out there in the towelling robe and demand the return of her own clothes?

The thought of getting back into them wasn't appealing and the underwear was really beautiful. She'd keep it and pay for it herself, get back into her jeans and T-shirt and go home.

Her determination to follow this path lasted until she walked back into the shop, which had now been closed and filmy curtains drawn across the windows. It could have been a film set, for Carlos lounged on the satin settee, while on a long table in front of him a platter of delicacies—dainty open sandwiches, breadsticks, cheeses and fruit—would have tempted even the most jaded of appetites, let alone a starving woman.

Marty joined him on the settee, conscious of her near nakedness beneath the robe—conscious of him so close.

'You can pay for this,' she said, waving her hand towards the spread as he passed her a glass of champagne. 'But I will pay for whatever I buy. Understand?'

'Of course,' he said, 'but it will not be nearly as much fun.'

Marty frowned at him, wondering about a trap, for he'd certainly given in too easily. But the food was wonderful and the champagne slipped like fizzy water so easily down her throat she let him refill her glass.

Maybe this was the trap—get her tipsy enough to not argue over who paid—but if she was too tipsy she wouldn't be able to try on the really beautiful clothes Ellen was now ferrying into one of the fitting rooms.

Setting down her glass, Marty concentrated on eating. Food would help allay the effects of the wine she'd already consumed.

And it *was* fun, she conceded later, if only to herself, as she pulled on pretty dresses then twirled in front of Carlos and Ellen in the privacy of the closed shop. Shoes had magically appeared in the dressing room, silly strappy sandals with bows and flowers, frivolous shoes Marty would never have thought of buying but which felt perfect on her feet.

Even the jeans and T-shirts Ellen produced were special— jeans that hugged Marty's body and made her legs look longer, teamed with printed T-shirts that were more wearable art than clothing. And when you added strappy sandals, jeans and a T-shirt, especially when worn to a barbeque, suddenly seemed the most exciting outfit in the world.

'I'll take these, two pairs of sandals, and that one dress in the bluey-green colour and the little skirt, and the other T-shirt and second pair of jeans,' she told Ellen, when the pile of tried-on clothes in the dressing room was reaching mountainous proportions.

'Dr Quintero suggests you wear the ones you have on, and he's already selected the other things.'

'It's none of Dr Quintero's business what I buy—he knows I'm going to pay for them and for the underwear so just tot up what the things I said I'll take will cost and put it on my card. Thanks.'

She picked up her little backpack and dug through it for her wallet, pulling out a credit card and praying the cost of the items of clothing she'd selected wouldn't shoot her credit limit up into the stratosphere.

'Dr Quintero said—' Ellen began, and Marty cut her off.

'I'm paying,' she said, pushing her card into the woman's hands.

Ellen stopped arguing and disappeared, and although Marty expected to have another argument with Carlos when she emerged from the fitting room, he said nothing, although his appreciative smile did funny things to her heart.

Ellen packed the modest collection of clothes Marty had bought into shiny bags, then handed Marty the credit slip to sign. The total made her blanch—it *would* make a huge dent in her credit limit, but she signed anyway, knowing she couldn't give back the super jeans and bright new T-shirts, while the skirt would be extremely useful and the dress—well, it had a floaty kind of skirt that flirted around her knees when she walked and the colour did something wonderful to her eyes…

CHAPTER SIX

'THAT *was* fun,' she conceded, as she walked out, Carlos carrying the bags.

'For me as well,' he said, looking down at her with an unreadable expression in his eyes. 'To see the transformation of Marty Cox.'

They walked in silence, but when they'd crossed the bridge and were on the last part of the river walk before they turned towards their separate homes, he edged her towards a wooden seat, set in the stone wall beside the path.

'You will tell me why you can't have children?'

The question was so unexpected Marty turned to stare at him, seeing the way one of the lamps shed light against his face so his profile was clear but his eyes shadowed.

No way to read a reason for the question, but she was beginning to learn he was a kind and caring man behind the mask of detachment he wore so well. He was also a doctor and, really, was it such a big deal? She just didn't normally talk about it, that's all.

Why not?

'I had always suffered bad cramps and abdominal pain, and my mother had suffered badly from endometriosis to the extent that her first child—that was me—was delivered by Caesar and she had a hysterectomy right then and there in the same theatre.'

'Giving your father no chance of having a son with her so he moved on?'

Marty stared at him.

'Did I tell you that?' she demanded, trying to remember when and why she'd have mentioned something she usually kept private.

'You were explaining your name—Martina!' he reminded her, taking her hand and holding it in his. 'Did your father leave immediately?'

'More or less,' Marty admitted. 'I never knew him—well, not as a father. He had no interest in me at all so Mum and I, it was always just the two of us.'

'Ah!'

'What's "ah" supposed to mean?' Marty demanded.

'Just ah,' the infuriating man said calmly. 'But you must admit it does tie into your belief you shouldn't marry. I imagine your mother didn't remarry for the same foolish reason you say you can't.'

'My mother didn't remarry because she was too busy working to support the two of us.' Marty knew she sounded defensive, but couldn't help it. 'My father paid a minimum amount of child support but my mother always thought that was *my* money and she banked every cent of it, using it eventually for my university expenses, for an old car when I needed transport, that kind of thing. And beside that, my reason isn't foolish!'

The only reply she got was a squeeze of her fingers and a velvety voice bringing her back to the original subject.

'So, you too suffered endometriosis?'

'Mum suspected it but, of course, it's not genetic, although I believe there could be a genetic predisposition to it. As I grew older, I had various investigations of it and treatment for it, but when I was twenty-three the pain was so severe I had to do something. I had lesions in one ovary and in tissue surrounding the uterus and made the decision to have a hysterectomy. I've kept the one ovary that wasn't affected purely for the benefits of producing some oestrogen but take tablets as well.'

She finished her recitation with a long release of breath—not really a sigh—then Carlos put his arms around her and drew her close, holding her against his chest in the most comforting embrace she could ever remember.

'Did you have counselling after the operation?' he asked, and she felt embarrassment heat her body, which had been thinking of things so far removed from the conversation it took her a moment to work out what he was asking.

'Counselling? No! I was through medicine by then, and had chosen a specialty, and I'd talked it through with friends, most of whom were doctors, so, really, I knew what I was doing.'

'Ah.'

Another 'ah' but this time she didn't ask him what it meant, knowing he was sure to tell her and not certain she wanted to hear it.

'Is it only since then you've hidden behind your clothing, downplaying a very shapely figure and your natural beauty?' he asked gently. He eased her back so one arm remained around her shoulders, while his free hand brushed through her hair, tousling it so the river breeze cooled her scalp. 'Was it that you were fearful of attracting men, knowing, as you told me last evening, that such attraction could lead to complications?'

He pressed her head against his shoulder, and Marty, quelling her natural urge, which was to argue with him, considered what he'd said.

'I'd prefer to think it was simply lack of interest that I haven't shopped for anything new for years, but if you want to go all psychoanalytical then I guess you might be right.'

His arm tightened momentarily.

'And has it never occurred to you that one day a man might want you more than he wants children?'

'No!' Marty said bluntly. 'Even dressed in fancy jeans and T-shirts, I'm hardly the kind of woman a man would lose his head over.'

'I wouldn't say that,' Carlos argued, and Marty shifted so she could look at him.

'You're not intimating you've lost your head over me, are you?' she asked, blunt as ever, yet disappointed when he shook his head.

'No, I wouldn't lie to you, Marty. I see you as a practical solution to my problems, but in my own way I am as damaged as you are—not that an inability to have children should be classed as damage, but it is obviously how you see yourself.'

'I might just sigh,' Marty said, bending over and gathering up the shopping bags he'd deposited at her feet.

He took them from her, carrying them the rest of the way but stopping when they reached her apartment building and handing them to her.

She read the message in the gesture—no strings attached—and knew the next move was up to her.

Come up for coffee? That's all she had to say, but the strong attraction she felt towards Carlos held her back.

'I need to think about a lot of things,' she told him, looking up into his face and watching his eyes for a reaction.

'I understand,' he said, then put his hand on her arm, steering her into the shadows of the leafy palm outside the entrance. 'Perhaps this will help you think.'

He bent his head and kissed her, not teasing her this time, not proving something, but firing a longing so deep and hot and hard inside her that her body trembled and she made little whimpering noises as she kissed him back.

The glossy bags slipped from her fingers and she locked her hands behind his head, needing support for a body that was melting into nothingness—reduced to boneless longing by the sexual power this man exerted over her.

She felt his hands explore her back, felt one move to cup a breast, and as her nipple peaked obligingly to the teasing of his thumb, she pressed harder against him, wanting and not wanting at the same time, her body betraying her with a hungry desire.

His lips, the smooth, hot taste of him, the slick black hair beneath her questing fingers, sensory exploration feeding her hunger to where she throbbed with need.

'As greedy as my daughter,' he said gently, when their lips had parted but were still only a breath away from touching.

'Only for your kisses,' she whispered, all restraint gone, all inhibitions vanquished, all self-restraint and common sense lost...

He lifted his hand and touched his forefinger to her lips, running it around their outline, firing her senses with even this so delicate caress.

'Your first decision, made before the kiss, was the correct one.'

He spoke softly, and though she reached out and grasped

his forearm, he did nothing more than press his hand against hers, before bending his head and kissing the little freckle at the corner of her mouth.

'You have to think about it,' he reminded her, 'but tomorrow—after we have been to Gib and Sophie's—do not expect such gentlemanly behaviour from me.'

Saturday morning, and a blissfully free weekend stretched in front of Marty. She woke early—it was a habit—then smiled when she saw the shiny bags, empty now, that she'd left in the corner of her room, thinking she might reuse them one day.

It *had* been fun.

And though Carlos had been honest enough about his reason for wanting to marry her, she'd noticed the gleam of appreciation in his eyes when she'd paraded in front of him—and had liked it!

Had more than liked the kiss that followed later.

Her body, remembering that heated encounter, shivered in the cool morning breeze.

Forget Carlos and kisses, she told herself, and sprang out of bed, pulling on not jeans but an old sweatsuit. She'd jog across the bridge then along the river path to Toowong and get the ferry back. That would take her mind off sex, and would take care of exercise for the weekend in case by some miracle she slept in tomorrow morning.

Or woke up in someone else's bed…

She definitely needed to get her mind off sex…

But as she ran, she thought not about the kiss but about what Carlos had said before the kiss—about her dressing down to hide away…

Was it true?

Had she subconsciously stopped buying clothes because she didn't want to be attractive?

'If that's the case, it's very sad,' she muttered to herself, making a couple passing on bikes turn to look at her.

But when she thought about it a bit more, she decided it hadn't been the case. Or not entirely! She'd been about to start specialising when she'd had the op, and that period of her life, with work and study, had been frantically busy, and since then she'd worked long and hard, building up her reputation, working her way up in the hospital hierarchy to where she was now one of the hospital's top O and G specialists.

Or had she worked so hard to replace the social life she hadn't believed she should have?

Damn the man for raising so many doubts. Her life had been so straightforward before this!

She rode the ferry back to South Bank, refusing to analyse herself any further, enjoying instead the quiet of the morning and the way the river slipped beneath the boat.

There was a note on her apartment door. Heartbeats that had calmed down on the ferry ride back to South Bank now accelerated, but it was from the building manager, asking her to call down and see him.

Obedient to a fault, she turned around and went back down to the ground floor where the manager had his home and office.

'Oh, Marty,' his wife greeted her. 'You were up early. A courier brought some parcels for you and as you weren't at home, he left them here. If you wait a minute, I'll get Des to help you carry them up.'

'I'm not expecting any parcels,' Marty said, totally mystified by what was going on, but one glance at the logo on the boxes and one glance at the shiny bags and she knew exactly.

But what to do?

Refuse to accept them?

Then they'd become Des and Jane's problem and that was hardly fair.

Carry them across the road and demand Carlos return them?

She could just see herself and Des in a procession of two, bearing them across the road to the classy hotel.

Outwardly meek but fuming inside, she gathered up what she could carry and, with Des following, returned to her apartment. Once inside she asked Des to put his burdens down on the living-room couch, then thanked him and saw him out. She went straight to the phone, but Carlos wasn't stupid.

'I'm sorry,' the woman on Reception said in her bland, hotel-polite voice, 'but Dr Quintero doesn't seem to be answering.'

Marty slammed down the phone, then wondered if he might be down in the café, having breakfast. She stormed out of her apartment, war on her mind, but by the time she reached the pavement outside her building her anger had faded at least enough to realise that tackling him in the café of the five-star hotel—he no doubt looking casually elegant as usual and she in sweaty and very likely smelly sweats—might not be the best idea.

She hesitated on the pavement then saw the picture. It was of a young woman with hair as short as her own, but the short hair in the picture was tipped with silver, making it look like fine spun glass around the young woman's head.

The picture hung in the window of a hairdressing salon, one Marty had occasionally frequented although there was also a place near the hospital that was more convenient for her.

Refusing to analyse her actions, she marched into the salon. Chances were they wouldn't have a free appointment on a Saturday morning.

'Only if you can stay now,' the young man told her. 'I came in early to do some bookwork but I hate bookwork. I'd much rather give you some tips.'

'Like the picture?' Marty asked, then felt pathetic. She was a grown woman, a professional, so why was she going all weak and feeble over a hairdo?

'Exactly like the picture, although I may use a little more gold in yours. You've a warm complexion, and lightly tanned skin and the gold will show up better.'

'I don't want to be a brassy blonde,' Marty warned him, and he laughed.

'I promise you won't be,' he said, leading her to a chair in front of a mirror then excusing himself to mix up what he'd need. Forty minutes of sitting in the chair with bits of foil standing up all over her head, then the dye was washed off, and Dave—an unlikely name for a hairdresser— worked some magic with a dryer, leaving a total stranger in the mirror.

'It's unbelievable!' Marty said, unable to hide her delight in her new image, but once she'd paid and left the salon, doubts crept in. Actually, they didn't creep, they rushed, swamping her with doubt. She was going to turn up at a staff barbeque with new hair and new clothes.

And *Carlos*!

What could any of her friends possibly think, except that she'd made herself over for him?

And hadn't she?

Good grief no! This had been a spur-of-the-moment decision made because she'd decided *not* to see Carlos this morning.

And there was still the little matter of the clothes.

She hurried back to her apartment, worried now that someone might see her before she'd thought it through. The message light was flickering on her answering-machine.

Carlos?

Not certain she wanted to talk to him, she ignored it for a moment, then knew she had to answer it.

'Marty, it's Gib. It's eight-forty and there's a problem with Emmaline—she's not sick or anything but still a problem. I've phoned Carlos and he's on his way and I thought it might be useful if you could be here as well.'

Marty's heart, which had stopped beating when Gib had mentioned Emmaline's name, dropped back to a normal beat, but anxiety twisted in her mind. What possible problem could there be?

She turned to leave the apartment, intent on getting up to the hospital as soon as possible, then glanced down at her attire and decided it didn't matter. It was already twenty minutes since Gib had phoned.

But her hair did matter. Fluffed hair and sweats! Not a good combination. On her way out the door she grabbed a baseball cap and pulled it down over her head, flattening the fluffiness Dave had created and hiding the tell-tale streaks.

'They're in Gib's office,' a nurse said, as Marty hurried into the NICU.

One look at the nurse's face had told Marty the situation was as serious as Gib's voice had sounded.

'Marty, it is good you are here!' Carlos greeted her, standing up and coming towards her to take her hands and draw her across to a chair. His eyes cast a quizzical glance towards her cap but she ignored it.

'What's going on?' she demanded, withdrawing her hands and nodding *yes* to Gib's offer of a coffee.

'Peter Richards is what's going on. He's being released from hospital on Monday and came up to the NICU, demanding to know whether his daughter would be able to leave with him.'

'His daughter? He's claiming Emmaline? When he never once visited either Natalie or the baby once he was mobile? I don't believe it.'

Marty cupped her fingers around the coffee-cup Gib had passed her, hoping the heat might spread from her hands and warm the coldness that had flooded through her body.

'He can't do it, can he?' she demanded. 'Can't take Emmaline?'

'We don't think so,' Gib said, 'but I've contacted a lawyer friend of mine to check into the legalities, and also asked a member of the hospital's legal team to come in to advise us on where we stand right now as far as keeping Mr Richards away from Emmaline. He says she's his child and because we can't prove how premature she was, we can't disprove his claim.'

'We can with DNA,' Marty protested, wondering why, if Gib and Carlos had already covered all this territory, Carlos wasn't joining in.

Or did he see Peter Richards's claim as a solution to his problem of what to do with Emmaline?

Much easier than marriage…

She put the coffee down in case her shaking hands sloshed it everywhere.

But could he really let Peter Richards—described by

a woman who'd *loved* him as a conman and no-hoper—take Emmaline?

Horrified by the thought, she glanced towards Carlos, but his face had assumed its mask-like look and she could read nothing in his stern features.

Or anything of the man who had fired her senses with a kiss less than twenty-four hours earlier.

'Carlos is not certain DNA is the answer,' Gib said quietly, shocking Marty into total immobility. But only for a moment, for one split second, before her temper blew.

'Of course it's the answer!' she said, far too loudly in that quiet, peaceful room. 'It will remove all doubt. Surely it's what the legal people will suggest. Emmaline's DNA matches Carlos's, and Peter Richards has no case.'

Silence from both men told her she was missing something and one glance at Carlos's face where stern had given way to a kind of anguish made her wonder just how far into her mouth she'd put her foot this time.

She sank back into the armchair and waited for someone to explain, but Carlos simply stood up.

'I am going to sit with Emmaline,' he announced. 'You might call me, Gib, when the legal person arrives.'

'So what's that all about?' Marty demanded of Gib the moment Carlos had left the room.

'I've no idea.' Gib shrugged helplessly. 'I raised the same point of DNA testing immediately after I'd explained about Peter Richards's claim and Carlos shut down completely.'

Marty hesitated but in the end had to voice her doubt.

'Do you think he wants Peter Richards to take Emmaline?' she said, her voice trembling with her own fear and uncertainty. 'I mean, he's seen her as a problem all along…'

'I don't know,' Gib told her, 'but I find it hard to believe that would be the case.'

The pair of them sat in silence for a while, but inside Marty the conviction grew that maybe Carlos *did* intend to give up his daughter, and with that conviction came a sick feeling of despair.

Beyond being attracted to him, she had actually grown to like Carlos, but now disappointment in her ability to judge a person joined the despair, to make her feel cold and nauseous.

Could she be that bad a judge?

It was no excuse that she barely knew him.

Barely knew him but had let her body be seduced by her attraction to him, to the extent she'd been imagining the bliss they'd share this evening...

She shook her head on the useless speculation and turned her attention back to the immediate problem of Emmaline. There was one obvious question that, as far as she knew, no one had raised.

'Why would Peter Richards want her?' she asked Gib.

'That's what worries me, and I think it worries Carlos as well. What possible reason could he have for wanting the baby, except that she *is* his child?'

'Can you tell how premmie she might have been? Did you ask Carlos the exact date Natalie left him? Is it possible Emmaline could be Peter's?'

'Yes to asking Carlos for a date and, no, I don't think Emmaline was premmie enough to be Peter's,' Gib replied. 'A baby of the gestational age he's talking about would have had gelatinous skin, and less well developed organs. And going the other way, Natalie and Carlos were together for six weeks, so she couldn't possibly have been pregnant by Peter when she met him—at least, not pregnant with Emmaline.'

'Then why is Carlos so dead against DNA?'

'Million-dollar question,' Gib said, and ran his hands through his hair in frustration.

'So what do we do?' Marty asked. 'Can we legally keep Peter away from Emmaline before there's some proof she's not his?'

'That's what I'm hoping the hospital legal person can tell me. It may involve making her a ward of the state and/or appointing a legal guardian for her.'

'Oh, no!' Marty said. 'Wouldn't that restrict other people's access to her?'

Gib smiled at her.

'I can always make you an honorary NICU doctor,' he promised, then a tap on the door interrupted them, and Gib hurried to answer it.

CHAPTER SEVEN

THE hospital legal person introduced himself as Dennis Swan, and Gib explained who Marty was, and why she was present.

'And the man you have, up till now, assumed was the baby's father?' Dennis asked.

'He's in the ward, with the baby. We call her Emmaline.'

'I see,' Dennis said, looking lawyerly and slightly disapproving, as if babies shouldn't have names until they had sorted out who their parents were.

'Perhaps you'll explain,' he said to Gib, who sat back down and proceeded to bring Dennis up to date with Emmaline's life thus far.

'You're certain it couldn't be the claimant's child?' Dennis asked, and Gib shook his head.

'I don't believe she could be, but there is only one way to be certain and that's DNA,' he told the lawyer. 'Unfortunately, Carlos—Dr Quintero—is reluctant to give permission for us to take blood from Emmaline for a test, and because, as far as we know, he is still the legal husband of Natalie at her death and as it's beyond dispute she bore the child, we have to consider him the parent and so need his consent for any procedure.'

'Have you spoken to Peter Richards about a DNA test? Has he agreed to one?' Dennis asked.

'I wasn't here when he came up to the NICU but was called in afterwards. By that time he was so angry it was impossible to talk rationally about anything.'

'Did you know of him before this incident? He has been in the hospital for some weeks. Had he made any previous claims or wanted to see the baby before this? Is there any evidence you know of that might prove his connection to the baby.'

'We know he was driving the car Natalie was in at the time of the accident,' Gib said. 'The car may have been in her name, but that proves nothing.'

'And he never once visited her, or the baby, before this, although he's been able to get around in a wheelchair for a couple of weeks,' Marty added.

But Gib, ever fair, excused him.

'A lot of people aren't good at visiting hospitals, and maybe seeing Natalie on life support would have been more than he could handle. We don't really know anything about him so we wouldn't know what he has or hasn't got. For all we know, he might have proof she was living with him—statements from neighbours or perhaps phone or electricity accounts in both names—but I can't see what else he'd have.'

'A letter from him appointing him legal guardian of the child should something happen to her?' Dennis suggested, and Marty felt her stomach turn and the nausea sweep back.

'Could he have that?' she whispered, afraid to contemplate such a scenario. 'And even if he has, would it count more than the legal rights of the father?'

'If we had DNA proof Dr Quintero is the father, we

wouldn't be discussing this right now,' Dennis pointed out. 'But if Mr Richards has such a letter, which, I might add, he claims to have, it would be up to the courts to decide.'

'He claims to have? You've already spoken to him?'

Dennis nodded.

'He demanded to see the hospital's legal representative immediately after he was denied access to the baby early this morning. I met with him before coming here.'

'But if he has this letter, why hasn't he produced it?' Marty demanded.

'He's been in hospital for six weeks and although his mother has been living in his apartment while he's been hospitalised, he claims she wouldn't be able to lay her hands on the letter because he's uncertain where he filed it away.'

'What he means is he hasn't forged it yet!' Marty said, her voice tight with fury, carrying clearly to Carlos as he re-entered the room.

She was a pint-sized fighter and he was pleased to think she was on his side, but when she noticed his return and turned on him, he wasn't quite so sure about the pleasure.

'Why on earth are you not settling this by giving permission for the DNA test?' she demanded, standing up, planting her hands on her hips and advancing towards him, angry fire from her eyes searing across his skin.

He hesitated for a moment, working out how to phrase what he wanted to say, then shrugged as if the matter was not of much importance.

'It may not be my legal right to give permission, and if I give it and it's not my legal right, we could well be in deeper trouble.' He wasn't certain of the legal accuracy of this pronouncement but it sounded good and right now he didn't want to think about, let alone talk about, his real reason for holding back.

He'd been watching Marty as he spoke so saw disappointment and something that looked like hurt wash across her face. Huge eyes looked up at him, then turned away as if unable to bear what they were seeing.

'You don't want her!' she said angrily, then she turned to Gib. 'And if that's the case, I can't see one single reason why I'm needed here. I may as well go home. I've got some things I need to return to a store.'

'Marty!'

The cry rang from his lips but she'd already stormed away, a small bundle of fury in a sweatsuit and a funny cap.

He stayed behind, talking to the lawyer, his mind on the woman who'd departed, a woman whose eyes had shone with delight as she'd paraded in the pretty finery last evening, then scorned him as she'd walked away today…

'I agree you might be getting into sticky territory, giving permission for the DNA test, although, as Natalie's husband at the time she died, you would be entitled to assume the child is yours.'

The child! It sounded so cold. Could the lawyer not call her by her name?

'Of course, we'd need to see some proof you were married to Natalie and check whether she'd started divorce proceedings, and we need dates of you meeting her and splitting up. I don't suppose the marriage was ever registered in Australia—that might cause more complications…'

Carlos had stopped listening, thinking instead of a tiny bundle with wild black hair and dark, dark eyes that had looked into his as he'd fed her.

Even if he could explain it, would a legal person understand his fear?

'Your marriage certificate?' Dennis prompted.

'I can get my lawyer to fax through copies of our
marriage document, but as far as I know I've not received
any communication from her since she departed.'

'As far as you know?' the lawyer queried.

'I've been working in Sudan and mail, when it gets
through, is hardly regular. My lawyer handles all official
correspondence. He has a power of attorney and takes care
of anything that comes up, simply advising me of any steps
he's taken on my behalf.'

'I shall need to speak to him,' Dennis said. 'Perhaps you
can make a time to phone him and explain the situation,
then be on hand should we need help with translation.'

'It is night-time over there—Friday night—and he's
likely to be out, but if we phone early this evening, it will
be morning in Barcelona and I will get him either at home
or at his office. We can phone from my hotel room.'

'I'll make sure my lawyer friend is there as well,' Gib
told Carlos. 'Dennis can't represent both you and the
hospital. She's coming to the barbeque and can bring you
along when you've finished your business.'

Dennis arranged a time to be at Carlos's hotel, and was
about to depart when Gib again raised the issue of keeping
Peter Richards away from Emmaline.

'You already have security on this floor and only those
people with passes around their necks are allowed in, but
perhaps you should get an extra security person up here
over the weekend,' Dennis suggested. 'I'll go down and see
Mr Richards and tell him he can't visit until the matter has
been resolved.'

He paused, turning to Carlos and adding, 'And perhaps, Dr Quintero, you will also refrain from visiting,' before walking out of the office.

Carlos thought of Emmaline, lying in her crib, and felt a physical pain run through his body.

Gib had seen some hint of this that he laid his hand on Carlos's arm and said gently, 'Don't worry. All the staff will give her extra attention and I know Marty will visit her as well.'

Marty!

Would she visit the baby she loved, or would the disgust she felt towards Carlos carry through to Emmaline?

Somehow he thought not. She was too fair in her dealings to be so petty…

The not petty person was stacking boxes and packages into a cab, her hands trembling with what she hoped was leftover anger and not regret.

'I want these delivered back to the boutique in the new arcade. The name's on the boxes, and tell the salesperson to credit them to the credit card that paid for them.'

The taxi driver looked at her as if she was speaking a foreign language, and after some more instructions she realised that, as far as he was concerned, she was. He was an immigrant who obviously understood street names and directions and could, no doubt, take fares to the airport or Central Station, but he hadn't a clue what she'd been talking about.

Marty opened the door again and climbed in, directing him to the city. She'd hoped to be spared this humiliation but, no, it was not to be. It took only minutes to reach her destination and she paid him, then tipped him to help her carry things inside. Fortunately Ellen was working, so Marty didn't have to explain too much.

'I did say I'd only take what I paid for,' she told the bemused woman. 'Now, please, can you credit all this stuff back to Dr Quintero?'

She marched out again, calm enough by now to notice her surroundings. The shop next door must be the source of the beautiful lingerie she'd bought the previous evening and, remembering the feel of the satin against her skin, she went in and indulged herself, buying four new bra and panty sets. She could wear them under her jeans and T-shirts and no one would know so no one would comment on the change in her.

Apart from her hair…

But if the rest of her hadn't changed, then hair wouldn't raise a comment.

Would it?

'Great hair!'

Her neighbour from the floor above greeted her when they met at the lift.

'Did you get it done at Dave's?'

Marty couldn't recall ever having a hair conversation, but she went along with it, agreeing Dave had done it then having to explain what colours he had used.

'I'm not up on this fashion stuff,' she muttered to herself as she unlocked her front door, but unfortunately the conversation and her thoughts had brought back Carlos's theorising of the previous evening. The one about her dressing down in order to avoid attracting men.

'Definitely psycho-babble!' she continued muttering to herself, and then, to prove him wrong even though he wasn't there, she marched straight into her bedroom and slid open the wardrobe doors.

She *did* have other clothes!

Well, she'd always known that—she'd just ignored that end of her wardrobe for the last few years.

How many years?

She pulled out a slinky dress she remembered wearing to a hospital ball, and seeing it remembered more.

Three years was the answer to her question. She'd worn this three years ago when she'd been going out with Larry Westwood, one of the pathologists at the hospital. She glanced along the rack and knew the other clothes on it hadn't had much of an airing for three years, although she had a couple of favourite skirts she wore when she and her mother went to a movie, as her mother believed one should make an effort to dress nicely when going out.

Jeans and Ts didn't cut it with her mother!

But the dress held her attention. A deep green silk satin that had sleeked down her body, making her look not tall exactly but certainly taller than she usually looked.

She'd been wearing it the night Larry had told her he'd met someone else—someone who could have his children. He'd come out with a six-pack of excuses—Marty'd always said she wouldn't marry him although he'd often asked, his mother wanted grandchildren, Marty's work was her life, he thought he'd make a good father, she put both her work and her mother in front of him, and Denise was happy to be a stay-at-home mother, something Marty, even if she could have had children, would never have been.

The moment he'd mentioned the name of the 'someone else' Marty had understood. Denise Swift had been a dazzling brunette with a very deep cleavage—usually on show—who'd been the talk of the hospital since she'd arrived as secretary to the pathology department. Every male on staff had found reasons to visit Pathology and although Denise had readily admitted to all and sundry that the largesse in her breast department wasn't all natural, it hadn't stopped the speculation on size, shape and texture.

Larry, apparently, had had no further need to speculate!

Marty hung the dress back up and flicked her fingers along the rest of the abandoned clothes. Some were out of date, but that pair of black trousers had always been a favourite, and somewhere—she rummaged through the shelf above the hanging space—she had a green knit top that looked great with them.

You could wear trousers to a barbeque…

Did she really want to go?

And if she did go, and wore trousers, would she be dressing for herself or for Carlos?

A man she didn't even like right now…

Yet again she considered sighing, but instead pulled all the clothes out of her wardrobe, flung them on the bed and began to sort them into 'still wearable' and 'op shop' piles. She had brave new hair, so why not a whole new image? And if she owed it to Carlos, well, too bad.

The phone rang as she was piling things into garbage bags. It was Sophie to say Carlos would be meeting with lawyers that evening and phoning his lawyer back in Spain to try to sort things out.

'Gib's lawyer friend will be with him and will bring him on to the barbeque if they finish in time, but I wanted to let you know you didn't have to bring him,' Sophie finished.

The disappointment Marty felt was totally out of proportion, considering how angry she still was over the DNA issue. But even not liking him, she'd been thinking of the ferry trip home, she in her black trousers and the green top that made her eyes look greener, he in whatever, both of them on the shadowy aft deck of the ferry, arms around each other, maybe kissing…

'I've got to get over this!' she said—loudly enough to startle a pigeon from her balcony. 'I've got to stop thinking about kisses. Not to mention what might follow kisses…'

The pigeon circled and landed back on her railing. Did pigeons understand human speech? Was he hoping she might go into details?

A second summons from the phone interrupted the pigeon train of thought.

'Mum! How was Scottish dancing?'

'Scottish *country* dancing,' her mother corrected, 'and it was wonderful. But as we didn't get together last night, what about coming to lunch tomorrow? I'll do a roast.'

Sunday roast! Something a woman living on her own never considered cooking just for herself. Marty accepted eagerly, promised to be there at twelve, said goodbye and hung up, only realising, after the connection was cut, that her mother still sounded inordinately cheerful.

Must be the dancing!

Marty was considering whether it might beat Tae Kwon Do for exercise as she packed away the rest of the clothes she'd been sorting. She'd grab some lunch, then have a leisurely shower, get dressed in her chosen 'going to the barbeque' outfit, and go up to visit Emmaline before catching the ferry to Gib's place on the river at Toowong.

* * *

The plan worked until she walked into the NICU and saw the young pregnant neonatologist Yui Lin, her usually placid face creased with anxiety, beside Emmaline's crib.

'A problem?' Marty asked, and Yui indicated the baby, whose tiny cheeks were flushed with fever and whose breathing was noisy and irregular.

'It happened so suddenly,' Yui explained. 'She was doing well enough for us to remove the heart and lung monitors then just an hour ago the sister on duty noticed she was breathing noisily. The sister immediately thought of hyaline membrane disease, but that usually shows up immediately after birth, not when a baby is a week old.'

'What else could it be?' Marty asked, knowing at this stage it was only guesswork but certain blood tests would be already under way in the pathology department.

'There's something called Wilson-Mikity syndrome,' Yui replied, 'that is rare but it sneaks up on you because it occurs in small, pre-term infants that haven't had HMD or mechanical ventilation. It's like an adult emphysema and can last several weeks or even months.'

Marty put her hand on Emmaline's tiny leg, distressed that the baby might be suffering and needing to offer some human contact.

'She looks feverish. Is fever a symptom?'

'Not really,' Yui said. 'Just respiratory distress, but the syndrome's so rare it's hardly ever diagnosed, with the result that we don't know much about it.'

Marty's stomach knotted at the thought of Emmaline with such a disease. Could a child who'd been doing so well suddenly develop something serious like this Wilson-Mikity thing?

'Let's get off rare,' Marty suggested. 'What else could it be?'

'Pneumonia,' Yui said, which didn't make Marty feel any better. Pneumonia could kill healthy adults, so how could so tiny a being fight it?

Determined not to let the other doctor see her fear, or the air transmit it to Emmaline, she gave a forced little laugh.

'Well, at least you can treat pneumonia,' she said. 'Whack some antibiotics into her and there you go.'

'If it is pneumonia,' Yui replied, squashing Marty's false cheer with four short words.

'How do you tell?' Marty demanded, sure something should be being done for the baby right now.

'We do X-rays but look…'

She used a remote control to turn on the light behind a light-box on the wall a little way from Emmaline's crib. 'Those cloudy areas are similar to X-rays of an infant with HMD, and although Emmaline's is unilateral, which is more common in pneumonia, it's still not enough for diagnosis. One of the problems is that all our babies, soon after birth, are treated with surfactants, which help the lungs transmit oxygen to the blood vessels, and the surfactants alter the appearance of the lungs so they can look like Emmaline's do.'

'So blood tests—swabs, how do you tell?'

'We don't,' Yui said soberly. 'Not for sure. Her blood cells show an increase in the white cell count but nothing significant, and throat swabs or sputum tests don't show much with neonates. But we will start her on broad-spectrum antibiotics just in case it *is* an infection of some kind, and keep watching her for further deterioration in her breathing which will happen if it's Wilson-Mikity.'

'And if it is?' Marty queried, though she already had a feeling she wouldn't like the answer.

'It's not fatal but there are long-term consequences— increased chance of bronchial diseases particularly during the first two years.'

In which case Carlos—or Peter Richards—would have a sickly baby to contend with—more problems ahead...

'It's very rare and we don't know for sure,' Yui reminded her.

Unsatisfactory though it might seem to Marty, she knew the difficulty of diagnosis in pre-term infants and that the team would have to work through a series of options in treating Emmaline.

'I'm putting her back into a humidicrib,' Yui continued, as a nurse approached with one of the covered cribs. 'That way I can give her more oxygen without putting her on ventilation.'

Marty watched as heart and lung monitors were once again attached to the tiny body, and Emmaline was returned to a humidicrib.

'It seems so unfair when she was doing so well,' she complained. Yui smiled in sympathy but shrugged her shoulders, obviously more used to these setbacks.

'You'd feel differently if it was your child,' Marty muttered as the other woman, pregnant with her first child, moved away, then she regretted taking out her own distress on the young doctor, even though she hadn't heard it. Yui was a great doctor and an asset to Gib's team.

The fact that Emmaline wasn't her child either didn't occur to Marty. Finding a chair to put beside the crib, she settled down to wait out the night. Barbeques and ferry trips forgotten, she slid her hand through the port and touched the little girl who'd come to mean so much to her.

Emmaline's condition worsened, her breathing raspy and her heart beating erratically as it battled to keep up an oxygen supply to the major organs of her body. At nine o'clock Yui phoned Sophie, who was Emmaline's prime carer.

'I didn't want to bring her in,' the young doctor explained to Marty, 'because it's the first weekend she and Gib have had off since their wedding, but I knew she'd want to know.'

Sophie, on arrival, agreed nothing more could be done, and that it was a matter of waiting for the drugs to work or for tests to show something different they might not have covered in the current treatment.

At two in the morning, the tiny baby girl turned the corner, her improvement obvious to the anxious staff who watched her, though Marty took longer to see that Emmaline was breathing more easily and her hectic colour fading slightly.

At four, Sophie told Marty to go home and get some sleep.

'She's over it now, whatever it was,' Sophie explained. 'I'm going to grab a nap in the on-duty room, and I promise I'll phone you if there's any change at all.'

Exhausted as much from the emotional drain as from a sleepless night, Marty stood up and stretched. She *would* go home and sleep, and hopefully wake up in time to get to her mother's for the Sunday roast, though that would depend on how Emmaline was doing in the morning.

If she had a relapse…

Marty's heart jittered at the thought, and she went into the washroom to splash cold water on her face and calm down before walking home. The make-up she'd put on for the barbeque had disappeared, although inevitably some mascara had leaked beneath her eyes. She scrubbed at it, then shook her head at the pale face looking back at her. The green top did make her eyes look greener, and the gold tips in her hair gave her skin a little colour, but she was still a plain Jane no matter what she wore or how she did her hair.

She left the washroom and headed for the lift, all but tripping over the long legs in the corridor.

'Carlos! What on earth are you doing here? Why are you sitting down? Are you ill?'

She knelt beside him, touching his shoulder, seeing the same drawn tiredness in his face that she'd grimaced at in her own only a minute earlier.

'Did you hear Emmaline was ill?' she asked, more gently now, her heart fluttering with uncertainty over how she felt about this man.

He straightened his back against the wall, then pulled his feet towards him and stood up, using his hand on Marty's elbow to help her to rise with him.

'I hope I didn't startle you,' he said, tugging at his shirt to straighten it. 'I sat down to wait and must have fallen asleep.'

'You sat down to wait?' Marty prompted.

'For news of Emmaline!' he said. 'We arrived at the barbeque to find Sophie had left because Emmaline was ill. I came at once. She's better now, or you wouldn't be leaving. Am I right?'

He'd gripped her hands as he'd spoken and his fingers tightened on hers with a fierce intensity.

'She's over the worst with her temperature down to normal and her breathing much easier. They're assuming it was pneumonia or a septic infection of some kind, and will keep her on antibiotics for seven to ten days.'

'Ah,' he said, and slumped back against the wall.

'Have you been here all night? Since you left the barbeque?' Marty asked, distressed by how exhausted he seemed.

'They told me not to visit her,' he said fiercely, nodding in reply to her question. 'They didn't tell me not to care.'

CHAPTER EIGHT

THEY didn't tell me not to care! The words echoed in Marty's head as she and Carlos walked home through the park. The summer days began early and the sky was lightening but they had the parklands to themselves.

Marty breathed the cool morning air deep into her lungs and pondered the meaning of those words. She'd sensed Carlos had been bonding with Emmaline yet his refusal to approve a DNA test seemed at best unconcerned, and at worst totally callous behaviour.

'You *do* care about her,' Marty finally stated, then waited for Carlos to deny it.

He didn't, but he didn't agree either, and, needing to know just what it all meant, Marty persevered.

'I know later you said it might not be your legal right to approve taking blood for a DNA test on Emmaline, but you'd said no to it before we got to discussing legal ramifications. Why?'

Still no reply, though a quick glance towards his face showed the grim mask back in place.

'It doesn't make sense!' she persisted, because walking with Carlos, tired though she was, had started all the physical attraction signals racing through her body, and she needed to know if her body could be so far wrong that it was attracted to someone who'd repudiate his daughter.

'Most things to do with emotion don't,' he said at last, pausing on the path and turning towards her. 'What makes sense with this attraction between us? You, who don't want a man in your life, and I, a chance-met stranger moving on at the end of the month. Yet we can't deny the attraction is there.'

He bent his head to kiss her, and Marty knew this was a diversion—something to stop her asking questions about his behaviour, to stop her digging deeper.

Then their lips met and her exhaustion was forgotten, the magic Carlos could produce within her body firing all her tired muscles with new life, and sparking heat along her nerves until her body burned with desire so hot she shivered as the river breeze brushed against her skin.

'You are cold. We should go inside. Your place or mine?'

Should she argue?

Deny the assumption he was making?

Ask again about the test?

He'd turned her in his arms and was walking, his hands still clasping her body, steering her along the path.

Hunger spiralled through her and she knew she wouldn't argue.

'Mine,' she managed, not adding that it was closer and she doubted she'd make the extra distance to his hotel without stripping off at least some of his clothing.

They started once inside her door, kissing again to find their rhythm, then Marty lost track of where she stopped and Carlos began as with a tangling of hands they undid buttons and lifted shirts and reached for skin to tease and learn and feel—to feed the fires.

Was his urgency as great as hers?

He growled beneath his breath when she touched him, then teased her to a whimpering need as his fingers flicked across her breasts. She kicked off her sandals—old ones, not new—as he eased his fingers into the waistband of her trousers, then moved so he could slide them down her legs, his mouth brushing against her navel as they slid lower, his tongue licking at her thigh while his hands eased the fabric off first one foot, then the other.

Now all that remained was a black silk thong, so slight and filmy it was no barrier to his demands, his mouth burning through the material as he licked and teased at the tiny nub of sensation beneath it.

'Bedroom?' he murmured as he straightened up, shedding his own slacks and underwear in one sweep, revealing his readiness in all its arrogant magnificence.

But it was too late to move, Marty shaking now with a need to feel him inside her, sliding off the flimsy panties, clasping his shoulders and fitting her body to his. With another growl, he lifted her, steadying her against the wall then holding her while she guided him into the hot, moist, aching centre of her being. She gasped as he filled her, crying out as her already sensitised flesh felt his firmness. Arousal rose and rose until it peaked with a suddenness that startled her and she splintered apart in his arms and collapsed against him, legs wound around his waist, arms clinging to his shoulders as he shuddered to his own climax then clasped her tight against his body, both of them slumped against the wall.

'Bed now, I think,' she managed to murmur, and he carried her through to the bedroom and put her down on the bed. Only this time he joined her, his hands turning her on her side so he could curve his body around hers and hold her while they slept.

Sure he wouldn't sleep, Carlos held the woman in his arms, and considered what had just occurred. Had she cast a spell on him, this small woman with the big heart?

That he, already burned by physical attraction, could let it tempt him again seemed impossible.

At least this time there'd be no unforeseen consequences...

But even as the thought occurred, he dismissed it as offensive. This woman in his arms was too fine a person for him to use comparisons with Natalie. This woman in his arms was unlike any woman he'd ever met before.

This woman in his arms...

He woke up to find her gone, though not far away, standing naked by the side of the bed muttering what sounded like 'Sunday toast'.

'You are upset?' he asked, pulling a sheet over his body to hide the fact it would be disappointed if she didn't come back to bed.

'I've got to go,' she told him, sliding open her wardrobe doors and peering distractedly at the clothes inside it. 'I've got to shower and dress and be at my mother's ten minutes ago.'

Obviously a crisis. Carlos forgot about a repeat session in the bed and rose to the occasion.

'You shower while I find clothes for you to wear. Does your mother approve of your jeans and T-shirt persona or does she prefer you to wear pretty things?'

Startled hazel eyes turned to stare at him.

'How would you know that?' Marty demanded, and Carlos laughed.

'I have a mother and two sisters. Of course I know. Now, go and have a shower. This Sunday toast, whatever it might be, must be important for you to be in such a state.'

'It's a Sunday roast, not Sunday toast—a meal,' she said, giggling as she disappeared into the *en suite* bathroom. 'And my mother always cooks enough for an army—you can't do small Sunday roasts. Would you like to come?'

Carlos heard the shower running and knew he'd have time to consider this casual invitation. That it was casual, he had no doubt. He also suspected Marty might be asking him in order to evade any recriminations about being late, though his own mother wouldn't hesitate to dress him down in front of company should she think he deserved it.

He was checking out Marty's wardrobe as he considered the invitation, and found a short white skirt with bright flowers on it and a dark teal top that looked as if it went with it. These he laid carefully on the bed, then searched opened drawers until he found the underwear.

Three sets of pretty, feminine frippery were laid on top of practical white cotton briefs and bras, and he smiled, wondering if the pretty ones were the result of their shopping expedition on Friday evening.

He chose a set in pale ecru lace and laid them on the skirt then, deciding he'd like to spend the next few hours with Marty, thinking about that sexy underwear beneath her clothes—anticipating the pleasure of peeling it off—he wandered into the bathroom to join her in the shower.

'There's no time for fooling around in here,' she said firmly, but her hands had touched his skin and fired his need again, so the Sunday roast would have to wait a while longer.

'If you don't mind me going in clothes I have slept in, I will come with you,' he murmured, when, sated once again, they stood beneath the water and he pressed kisses to her ear and whispered his decision.

'My mother won't know you slept in your clothes. I'll call us a cab.'

She slipped away, and Carlos watched her go, wondering about this woman who was so unabashed about the new relationship in which she found herself, treating it as the natural happening it probably was, without embarrassment or coyness or recrimination.

He found her small razor and did his best to remove the overnight stubble, wondering as he scraped away at it if he'd scratched her in their love-making.

By the time he emerged into the bedroom, she'd laid his clothes out on the bed where he'd put hers earlier. He dressed and joined her in the living room, waiting by the door as she finished a telephone conversation.

'I phoned the NICU—Emmaline's continuing to improve. Gib and Sophie have both had a look at her, and think it was an infection.'

'So we can eat our Sunday roast without concern,' Carlos said, but apparently Marty didn't agree.

'I don't know about that. Look at me! My eyes are sparkling and my skin's all flushed, although that could be beard burn. One look and my mother's going to guess we've been in bed together.'

'Is that so bad?' Carlos asked, following her out to the lift. 'If you like—if it would make things easier—I will not come.'

'Don't you dare pull out at this stage,' Marty told him, taking his hand and hauling him into the lift, as if he might escape. 'At least with you there she can only surmise, and I'll get the questions some other time. What really gets to me is that I've gone into an affair with a man I'm not sure I like.'

She looked directly at him, her eyes as challenging as her words.

'Because you feel you do not know me?'

'Because of the DNA thing. You diverted me off that subject earlier—and diverted me very nicely—but it bothers me, Carlos.'

His eyes lost the soft glow that was the aftermath of loving, then were quickly shuttered against her, his eyelids dropping to hide any expression they might have revealed.

'It is a legal decision,' he said bluntly, and though she didn't believe it, she knew it was the only answer she would get, as they 'd reached the ground floor and the cab was waiting outside the front door.

She pretended it didn't matter, and held his hand as they sat in the back of the cab, telling him about the suburbs through which they were driving.

'I normally get the ferry to St Lucia, near the university, and walk to Mum's place from there, but because we're late…'

He squeezed her fingers and she glanced towards him, wondering what on earth he must be thinking and why he'd agreed to come to lunch with her mother. She knew why she'd asked him—not to waylay her mother's questions, that was an excuse. She'd asked him because she loved him—a blinding insight that had occurred to her in that moment in the corridor outside the NICU when he'd stood up and said, 'They didn't say I couldn't care.'

Right then and there she'd experienced a rush of feeling unlike anything she'd ever felt before, and though she had nothing in the past with which she could compare such a force, she'd recognised it as love.

Not that she could tell him—nor even think clearly

about it herself. Not when it was so new, and now muddled up with the physical attraction and the sexual delight she'd experienced earlier.

Not to mention the 'not liking him' conundrum!

'The next house on the right,' she told the cab driver, inwardly anxious now about this visit and her decision to bring Carlos. What if her mother leapt to the wrong conclusion? Thought there was something serious between them?

Had Carlos felt her tension that he squeezed her fingers once again, helped her from the cab, paid the driver, then dropped her hand so she could lead the way into the small house where she'd grown up.

But any concerns about how her mother would view the situation were banished the moment she opened the front door and, calling out a hello, walked into the house. The smell of sizzling lamb filled the air, but there was another scent, unfamiliar to the house, that caught Marty's attention.

'Your mother smokes a pipe?' Carlos asked, as Lucy Cox came through the living room to embrace her daughter.

'Mum, this is Carlos Quintero, a visiting doctor at the hospital. Carlos, my mother, Lucy Cox.'

'Oh!' Lucy said, looking up at Carlos for a moment before remembering her manners and holding out her hand. 'How do you do? I'm so glad Marty brought you.'

But Marty's attention was no longer on introductions. It was focussed on the source of the pipe smoke—a large man standing on the deck beyond the living-room windows.

'Come and meet Alec,' Lucy continued, and, totally bemused, Marty followed her mother out to the deck.

'Alec, this is Marty.'

Marty was aware her mother was introducing Carlos to the man, but her mind was still trying to assimilate the fact that her mother had a man friend. She wasn't upset—in fact, she rather thought she might be pleased—but right now shock was her major emotion and it seemed to have disabled her brain so all she could do was offer her hand, mutter something she hoped was polite, then stand back and let Carlos take up the conversation.

Which, to her great relief, he did, answering her mother's question about where he was from, and launching into a lengthy description of his work in war-torn Sudan.

'So a lot of your patients would have bullet wounds,' Alec said.

'Or shrapnel wounds from home-made bombs and grenades. It's patch-up medicine most of the time, but between bouts of warfare we do have peace, and it's during that time we try to get as much preventative medicine done as we can. Vaccinations, information on the importance of clean water and proper rubbish disposal, talking to mothers about child care, teaching the rudiments of first aid.'

As he spoke Marty felt again the urge to work in some of these places, helping people who had so little. She looked speculatively at the man called Alec and wondered if maybe he represented an opportunity for her to do just that.

'Come and help me serve,' her mother suggested, and Marty was only too willing to follow her into the kitchen, leaving the two men on the wide deck that hung above a fern-filled gully.

'So?' she demanded of her mother, as Lucy turned to her and used the identical word.

Marty waved away her mother's 'So?' with a casual, 'He's just a colleague from overseas, working with me for a while. I thought it would be nice for him to meet someone outside the hospital.'

'And I'm a super-model!' her mother teased, 'but if you don't want to talk about it, that's OK because I do want to talk about Alec. It's why I wanted you to come today.'

And as Marty took in the flush on her mother's cheeks and the shine in her eyes, she felt a mixture of happiness and loss—happiness for her mother who'd been alone for so long, yet loss for the relationship that they'd always had and would now, inevitably, change.

But as her mother explained how they'd met, and described her delight at falling in love a second time, Marty could only feel pleased, for if anyone deserved a second chance at happiness it was her mother.

She waited until the roast had been removed from the oven and set safely on the kitchen bench before hugging the older woman and telling her how glad she was.

'I'm glad you're glad. I was worried,' Lucy admitted. 'You've had such a rough time with love yourself, I wondered if you'd understand.'

It took all the roast's resting time for Marty to convince her mother of her genuine pleasure at the news, and by the time the meat was cut and the vegetables served, she was looking forward to learning more of the man who had brought such happiness to her mother.

'He is an interesting man,' Carlos remarked, as they walked from the house down towards the river much later in the afternoon.

'He is,' Marty agreed, but must have sounded less than enthusiastic, for Carlos put his arm around her shoulders and drew her close.

'It worries you, this man coming into your mother's life?'

Marty shook her head.

'I couldn't be happier for her.'

Carlos stopped walking and turned her to face him.

'Then why are you sad?' he demanded and she had to smile at his percipience.

'Not sad, exactly. Not sad at all, because I'm happy that they've found each other. It's just…I suppose melancholic is the only word because things have changed. For so long, it's been just Mum and me—pathetic though that sounds coming from a thirty-year-old woman, and silly, because we've each lived separate lives for a long time, but it's still there, this funny feeling that now things will be different.'

Carlos wrapped his arms around her and hugged her.

'Life is all about change,' he reminded her, and they walked on.

The ferry trip back to South Bank was all too short, Marty pointing out Gib's house on the river, which Carlos had visited briefly the previous evening.

'And that reminds me,' he said, glancing at his watch. 'I have a meeting again this evening with Lisa.'

His arm had tightened around Marty's shoulder as he'd said it, but she'd still felt alarm that Gib's lawyer friend should be a woman, especially as it meant she and Carlos had to part once again outside her building, she to go home alone while he returned to his hotel room to shower and change in time to meet the lawyer for dinner.

'But later?' he said, sounding tentative for the first time since she'd met him.

She smiled and kissed his cheek.

'We'll have other times,' she reminded him. 'You see the lawyer and sort things out for Emmaline. I've a couple of on-call nights this week and need to catch up on my sleep.'

But the sense of loss she felt as he walked across the road, turning on the far footpath to raise a hand in farewell, was out of all proportion to their relationship—such as it was.

Was this what love did to you?

Made every parting harder?

And could it really be love, given her doubts about him as a person?

Yet Natalie had apparently loved her no-hoper, even knowing him for what he had been.

Inexplicable, that's what love was—just look at her mother and Alec.

Thoughts on the mysterious ways of love took Marty up to her apartment, but once there she set them aside, her mind returning to the twin puzzles Peter Richards's bombshell had raised—Carlos's refusal to give consent for a DNA test on Emmaline and, even stranger, why Peter Richards would want the baby.

She made herself a drink and went into the spare bedroom, which she used as an office, settling down in front of her computer.

It was a bit of a stretch but not entirely unreasonable to suppose Natalie might have chosen to keep the baby to get money out of Carlos. Carlos himself seemed to think that could have been possible so presumably he had money apart from the pittance he would earn in Sudan. But what could Peter Richards gain from having Emmaline now Natalie was dead?

Had he been so in love with Natalie he wanted something to remember her by? Wanted her child?

If that was the case, wouldn't he have visited her when she was in the ICU? Exhibited some sign of grief when told of her ultimate death?

Pleased to have something to keep her mind off Carlos

and his female lawyer and the DNA problem, Marty ran a search on Peter Richards's name, and once she found the right one discovered the number of cons he'd pulled, the jail time he'd served and the sentences that had been suspended. All his tricks were based around separating people from their money, with funds supposedly going into miracle cures for cancer or a plantation of drought-resistant cattle feed or, in one case, a yabby farm. Again and again the schemes had failed, but Peter Richards had come out of every one of them with money.

So what had he in mind for Emmaline?

CHAPTER NINE

SHE was no nearer to finding an answer to this or the love problem when she left for work the following morning, although the ache in her heart when she realised Carlos wasn't perched on the edge of the planter outside her front door suggested love wasn't all it was cracked up to be.

Why should he be there? Marty demanded of herself as she stomped grumpily along the path towards the hospital. It wasn't as if she'd been exactly welcoming last night when he'd suggested coming over after the dinner with his lawyer.

'That was different,' she muttered, startling a mild-looking businessman walking in the opposite direction.

But no matter how firm the talking to she gave herself, the ache she felt at his absence persisted, accompanying her on her ward round, unalleviated by the joy of five new mothers who proudly showed off the latest additions to their families.

Though at least as far as work was concerned, all was well.

No problems, no hassles—but experience warned Marty this could not last.

It didn't—the call to report to A and E came just before she was due to go to lunch.

A and E—Carlos! Pathetic leap of her heart, though she didn't know for sure he'd be there.

'Twenty-year-old primigravida, thirty-six or -seven weeks pregnant, developed dizziness, some aphasia and increasing ataxia over the last few weeks,' the admitting nurse at the desk reported to Marty, who liked to know all she could about the patient's condition before meeting her.

'Hypertension?' Marty queried, thinking of pre-eclampsia, a condition potentially dangerous for both the mother and the child.

The nurse shook her head and checked her notes.

'BP 120 over 70, not bad at all. FHR strong, we've put a foetal heart monitor on her.'

'I think it is not pregnancy related,' a now-familiar voice remarked, and Marty, her heart fluttering with totally unnecessary excitement, turned to see Carlos right behind her.

Resisting the urge to touch him, she looked into his face, but it was as if their closeness of the previous day had never been, his features wiped clean of all expression, except for a certain grimness she suspected was not to do with their patient.

He nodded, all cool professional, towards the notes the nurse had handed Marty, but didn't explain.

Well, she could out-professional him any day!

'You have an idea, Dr Quintero?'

He took a step back, as if she'd hit him, but his face remained impassively unreadable.

'I called a neurosurgeon while the nurse called you. He was already in A and E and has seen her,' he explained. 'He has suggested a CT scan of her head. The symptoms of a lack of co-ordination of the voluntary muscles suggest a problem in the cerebellum—perhaps a tumour of some kind.'

'Have you contacted Radiology?' Marty asked, agreeing that the symptoms did suggest a problem in the patient's brain rather than a pregnancy-related cause, worrying now about the pregnant woman, not her own foolish reactions to this man.

Carlos nodded. 'The neurosurgeon has arranged it. The patient is actually on her way to Radiology now.'

'Do you have a history?' Marty asked, surprised at how easy it was to talk to Carlos about medical matters, in spite of this sudden coldness he was exhibiting towards her.

What was less easy was how she felt when close to him—how her body wanted to lean in towards him and her fingers yearned to touch the skin on the inside of his wrist, or slide into the silky darkness of his hair...

He was already answering her, explaining how the young woman's boyfriend had noticed her stumbling from time to time as long as six weeks ago. She had apparently laughed it off, putting her clumsiness down to the extra weight she was carrying, but then her speech had shown signs of stuttering and she'd begun to lose words.

'She started having dizzy spells then this morning passed out altogether and he really panicked, bundling her into the car and driving her straight to the hospital.'

'Did they visit a doctor at any stage?'

Carlos shook his head.

'When you see the boyfriend, you will understand. They believe in natural remedies. They have read up on natural childbirth techniques and were hoping to bring their child into the world with only themselves and some of their friends involved.'

'Which would probably have worked if there were no complications,' Marty said, then she turned as a neurosurgeon she knew came into the open area at the back of the A and E department.

'You've seen the pregnant woman's scans?' she asked, as the man greeted her and then Carlos.

'She has an astrocytoma invading the cerebellum,' he told her. 'It may still be benign but it's the type of tumour that can develop a highly malignant glioblastoma within the tumour itself. Although it's slow growing, it's obviously causing problems for the patient to be passing out, and if we don't operate *a.s.a.p.* it could cause permanent brain damage.'

'You'll operate now?' Marty asked, thinking of the baby the woman was carrying and the complications a long time under general anaesthesia could cause.

'After you,' the neurosurgeon said, touching the back of his head and smiling at her. 'Bit hard to open up the back of her skull when she can't lie flat on her stomach.'

'So we do a Caesar then you keep her in Theatre and do the brain tumour? Have you spoken to her partner?' Marty asked, wondering if she'd ever stop learning things in her chosen profession.

'No, that's why I'm here, to speak to him and to you. You'll do the Caesar?'

'I will and I'll call up to the NICU—if she's only thirty-six weeks we'll need a neonatal team in Theatre to take the baby. But the main concern must surely be the mother. Will she be all right? Do you think there could be permanent damage already?'

'I doubt it. Her reflexes are good. Now, I've already arranged for the woman to be taken to Theatre and I have an anaesthetist standing by with the pre-op drugs, so who do we see to get permission for this?'

'She's not conscious? Can't give permission?' Marty looked from the neurosurgeon to Carlos then back to the surgeon.

But it was Carlos who answered.

'She hasn't regained full consciousness since she passed out at her home. She has roused briefly a few times and tried to speak, but generally she's been close to comatose.'

He spoke gently, but fear for the woman, and for her baby, gripped Marty's heart. Could the woman be unconscious for so long and *not* have brain damage from the tumour? Would the tumour be benign? Could the baby lose its mother within hours or maybe months of its birth?

'Your job is to deliver a healthy baby,' Carlos said, so gently Marty wondered if he'd read her mind. Then he took the neurosurgeon through to the waiting room to find the young man and explain what was happening.

And hopefully get permission for the two operations.

'He's agreed, but is so distressed that his girlfriend won't be conscious for the birth, I've phoned a friend of his to come and sit with him.'

Carlos explained this when he joined Marty in the scrub room of the chosen theatre, explained it in a voice that told her not to question him about anything personal—not to ask what had happened to change things between them so much.

'He could be here for the Caesar,' Marty said, pretending to be as unconcerned by this change as Carlos obviously was, although inside she was beginning to feel sick. How could she have thought herself in love with someone who could change so much in twelve hours—who spoke to her as if he was nothing more than the colleague he had started out to be?

He was shaking his head in reply to her question.

'He says it would not be fair for him to see the baby born and his girlfriend not see it. Her name is Summer, and he asked that we use it to her even if she cannot hear.'

Marty nodded, accepting his words if not his manner. She, who'd talked to Natalie for weeks, certainly understood that!

But as she headed into Theatre she set aside her own concerns and focussed totally on Summer, and on the operation ahead, running through in her head what she would do. The woman was young, so a low transverse incision would be best, keeping it as small as possible so the scar would be barely noticeable later and the muscles would regain full strength so Summer could deliver vaginally if she had another child.

She nodded to Yui Lin, the neonatologist from the NICU, and the two support staff she had with her. They had set up their portable resuscitation trolley in a corner of the theatre and would take the baby and stabilise him or her as soon as Marty delivered it.

One of her own theatre sisters was on hand for this first part of the operation, and she had the instruments and a baby bundle already set out, the bulging stomach draped and the skin prepped so Marty could begin.

Explaining, for Carlos's sake, as she operated, she cut through the skin and muscles of the abdominal wall, exposing the peritoneum, the membrane that enclosed all the abdominal organs. Carefully, she cut through that, clamped it open, then eased the woman's bladder to one side to expose the swollen uterus. Another transverse cut, but this time a very short one, into which she slid her fingers so she could stretch the opening wide enough to see the foetal sac and enable her to cut the membranes of the sac and feel inside for the baby's head.

'I use forceps to ease it gently out, and the anaesthetist, once the head is out, administers a dose of oxytocin, which is a natural hormone, to the mother. This will help the uterus contract and also help prevent extensive bleeding.'

She delivered the rest of the baby, a not so small girl, holding her upside down while the neonatal respiratory technician suctioned the mouth and nose, then Marty grabbed a cloth from the baby bundle, wrapped the infant and handed the baby girl to Carlos.

'Emmaline arrived just the same way. Hold her while I deliver the placenta and we cut the cord then you can take her over to the trolley and watch the neonatal team check her out.'

But Carlos had stopped listening. He was holding the baby as carefully as he would a priceless but very fragile treasure, and was smiling down at her, telling her what a clever girl she was and that everything would be all right.

This was the Carlos, Marty realised, with whom she'd been foolish enough to fall in love.

The other Carlos—the one she'd met today and who had refused the DNA test—was a stranger.

She watched as he handed the baby to Yui, then dismissed him from her mind, wondering instead about the reassurance he'd given the baby girl.

Would everything be all right? she wondered as she finished stitching up the wounds she had made, dressing them then leaving her patient for the neuro team. It could be five or six hours before they finished, and even longer before test results on the tumour came through.

Would Summer's baby have a mother or, like Emmaline, would she never know the woman who had given birth to her?

A sadness so deep it seemed to leak out the pores of her skin overwhelmed Marty, and though she'd intended visiting Emmaline in her lunch-break, she knew she couldn't lest she affect an innocent child with her mood.

She went down to the canteen instead, knowing her body needed the fuel food would provide, although it was now closer to afternoon tea than lunch. The first person she saw was Carlos, sitting with a long-haired young man and an older, kindly looking fellow with a thick beard. She nodded to him and would have walked past but he gestured to her to come across, and introduced her to Kevin— Summer's partner—and his father, Mike.

'Have you heard how they're getting on?' Kevin asked anxiously.

'No, but that doesn't mean anything,' she said. 'It's a tricky operation—anything involving the brain always is. But this type of tumour sends tentacles into the tissue and each one of those has to be teased out and removed without doing any damage to the brain itself.'

'And if it's malignant?'

Marty heard the fear in his voice and sat down beside him, resting her hand on his shoulder.

'I'm sure Dr Quintero has already told you these tumours are rarely malignant in themselves. They are slow growing and sometimes the person has to have more operations maybe years later to remove new bits of them, but, given Summer's age, it's unlikely to be malignant.'

She prayed that she was right, but even if she wasn't, there was nothing to be gained from Kevin being more worried than he already was.

'Have you seen your daughter?' she asked, to change the subject of the conversation, then was surprised when he shook his head.

'I don't want to see her before Summer does,' he said

softly. 'We had this all planned, how we'd both see her together, and we'd say her name, Wind Cloud, so she'd know straight away who she was. If it was a boy it would have been Storm Cloud, but I'm glad it's a girl. I think Summer secretly wanted a little girl.'

Marty hugged his shoulder.

'I think what you're doing, not seeing the baby until Summer can, is wonderful,' she said, her voice tight with emotion as pity for the young couple in trouble threatened to swamp her.

She stood up.

'I've got to get something to eat,' she said, moving away, but Kevin caught her hand.

'Thank you,' he said quietly, squeezing her fingers with a gentle pressure. 'And thank you, too, Carlos, for all you said about responsibility.'

Carlos nodded and stood up, joining Marty as she moved away.

'I too was on my way to eat when I saw Kevin and his father. Shall we eat together?'

He sounded uncertain of his welcome, which, Marty felt, given his attitude towards her this morning, he should be.

'Are you sure you want to?' she demanded, unable to hold back the hurt any longer.

He held out his hands in a helpless gesture.

'I should have phoned or walked to work with you but, Marty, I am so confused I would have been a burden you did not need or deserve. You have shown me nothing but kindness and given yourself to me so freely—so beautifully. How could I spoil that by bringing you despair?'

'What's happened?' Marty demanded, stopping dead in the middle of the canteen and staring up at him.

'Peter Richards has the letter,' he said, his eyes so full of hurt Marty wanted nothing more than to put her arms around him and rock his body against hers to ease his pain.

But he'd distanced himself from her, and although the reasons he'd given her sounded altruistic, Marty couldn't help wondering if it was his way of disentangling himself from what could have become an awkward situation.

She stepped backwards before she could give in to temptation.

'Lisa showed me a copy of it last night. She is uncertain how much weight it will carry legally, but it certainly states that Natalie wished Peter Richards to be the guardian of her unborn child.'

'But is it a legitimate document? Can he prove Natalie actually wrote it?'

He touched his finger to her lips.

'Does it matter? Those are exactly the kind of questions that could put Emmaline's future in limbo for many years to come. Proving this, disproving that, getting cases into court, let alone fighting them. Is this fair on her? How will this affect her?'

Marty stared at him in disbelief.

'You'd give her up to him?'

'I didn't say that,' Carlos growled, 'and this is hardly the place to be discussing it.'

'Well, I don't know of anywhere better. Your daughter is five floors above us, recovering from an infection that has knocked her for six, and you're talking about legal ramifications!'

Carlos took her elbow and steered her towards the self-service food cabinets.

'You would prefer she become a ward of the state and

be fostered out to total strangers while this is sorted out?' he growled.

'No! I'd prefer you to have taken a DNA test and given permission for blood to be taken from Emmaline for comparison so you could have sorted this thing out once and for all. And don't bother telling me you couldn't legally give permission—the hospital lawyer only agreed with you over that after you put the idea into his head.'

Carlos didn't answer, his hands busy stacking plates of food onto a tray though Marty thought she could detect a slight tremor in his fingers—fingers that had worked magic on her body the previous morning...

'You can't possibly eat that much,' she finally told him as he loaded two highly calorific desserts onto the already laden tray, and the silence had gone on too long for her to bear it.

'You need to eat—you could be called upon to operate on someone or deliver a baby. I don't know what you want to eat but at least this way you'll have some choices.'

He pushed the tray along the counter, herding her in front of him, until he reached the checkout.

'Two long blacks,' he told the young man behind the till, who was eyeing the array of food with startled fascination.

'I mightn't have wanted coffee,' Marty grumbled.

'I mightn't have wanted a baby,' he retorted, stirring the embers of Marty's anger once again.

'It's not the same thing!' she fired at him as he paid the young man and picked up the tray, now with two cups of coffee added to the precarious load.

'No, it's not, but the fact remains that in this life we don't always get what we want.'

And Marty didn't need the ache in her heart to tell her just how true that was.

Carlos carried the tray to a table in the far corner of the canteen and prayed Marty wouldn't be paged until he'd said what he wanted to say to her.

The argument they'd just had wasn't exactly a propitious start, but he knew she was sensible enough to put her doubts about him to one side and consider his proposition with a clear mind.

Perhaps he should amend that to he *hoped* she was sensible enough.

He took the plates off the tray, passed one cup of coffee to Marty and arrayed the rest of the food he'd selected down the centre of the table so she could choose what she wanted for herself.

'Eat!' he ordered, and though she looked at him and raised her eyebrows at his order, she did reach out for a plate of sandwiches, all her attention focussed on removing the plastic wrap. Deliberately not looking at him?

He took a plate of sandwiches himself, selected one and bit into it. It tasted like sawdust, but he knew he had to eat. Drank some coffee with it—dishwater and sawdust— pushed both aside and studied the woman across the table.

It was hard to believe so wide a canyon of mistrust and uncertainty had widened between them, when yesterday they had been as one.

His blood thickened at the memory of their love-making but he ignored his body, his mind bent on putting his proposition to Marty in such a way she might just agree to go along with it.

'I would like us to marry.'

That wasn't quite how he'd meant to phrase it, and earlier, when he'd considered the idea, he'd meant to lead up to it with words about not love but liking, and respect, and affection. But their argument had him on edge and the knots in his gut when he thought of Emmaline had made him blurt it out.

She didn't answer, though she did turn her attention from her sandwiches—were hers also tasting of sawdust that she had taken a bite out of three of them before setting them back on the plate?—to him.

She stared at him for a moment, then her forehead puckered in a frown.

'You would like us to marry?' she said in such incredulous tones he felt aggrieved.

'I did suggest it once before,' he reminded her.

'I thought you were mad then and this just confirms it. You buy a heap of food, plonk it down on the table, sit yourself down and tell me you'd like us to marry. You *have* to be mad!'

He wanted to reach out across the table and take her hand—to hold it as he tried to explain. Ideally, he would like to be in bed with her, holding her body tucked against his, murmuring these things in her ear.

Although that might be cheating...

'The situation is not of my making,' he said, knowing he sounded ridiculously stiff but unable to prevent his tension leaking into the words. 'But it is urgent, so there is no time to woo you with flowers and gifts and fancy words. Lisa feels if I am married, and married to an Australian woman, it might expedite the case, or at least allow me to have Emmaline in my care until such time as the courts make a decision.'

He glanced across the table to see how his chosen wife was taking this explanation, but her blank expression suggested she was so shocked by it her mind had ceased to think, so he pushed on, hoping further explanations might help her.

'Lisa said there is a waiting period of one month for marriage, which is too long, but which can be reduced in special circumstances. We would qualify as special circumstances and she offered, just to help me out, of course, to marry me herself.'

'Just to help you out, of course,' Marty muttered, her eyes darting fire hot enough to turn the sandwiches to toast.

'It was a legal kind of offer,' he tried to explain, although Lisa's rather bizarre suggestion had startled him as well.

'I bet it was!' Marty retorted.

'Lisa's offer is not the matter under discussion,' Carlos told her, desperate to get the conversation back on track. 'You love Emmaline—will you not do this for her?'

'That's playing foul, Carlos!' Marty said, and he wondered if the sudden brightness in her eyes was caused by withheld tears.

'It's how I have to play. Her future is at stake here, Marty. Would you prefer to see her made a ward of the court and put in foster-care?'

'As against me taking her home with me while you swan off to Sudan? What am I supposed to do? Give up my job to care for her? She's a baby, not a package you can leave in a luggage locker somewhere when it's inconvenient to have her around.'

'You will not give up your job. I will arrange a nanny for her and accommodation and whatever else you need, and if this cannot be done before I am due to return to Africa, I shall stay and care for her myself.'

Marty stared at him, unable to believe they were having this conversation at all, totally unable to believe where it had led.

'You would stay and care for her yourself?'

He nodded, then said quietly, his voice riven with emotion, 'She is my daughter.'

How to breathe when he'd made such a statement, and her heart had stopped its beating? Marty held herself very still, willing her body to return to normal. She thought of the baby she loved, held in some limbo while courts decided her fate, and knew she couldn't deny the tiny girl this chance to go to a home where she'd be loved.

But where would such a rash, short-term solution leave her?

What would happen long term?

She studied Carlos's face, seeing the strong features and the slightly stern expression it had even in repose.

Marry him?

Fall more deeply in love with him, then what?

Be left with nothing but a lonely bed and a broken heart…

Or was there a possibility she'd have Emmaline? That once legal guardianship was determined, she might be able to adopt Emmaline as her own?

That at least would be some solace, but she was damned if she'd get a nanny. She was due some long-service leave—she'd take that, maybe study while she was at home and take up a teaching position for a few years until Emmaline was old enough for school.

Stop right there! The order came down from some still rationally functioning cells in her brain. Emmaline is not the issue right now, this marriage is, and when you think about it, if Carlos is willing to go this far to gain custody of his child, why would he then be willing to hand her over to you?

'It would be a marriage of convenience? Just until the legal ramifications are sorted out?'

She was watching him closely so saw the flicker of surprise that crossed his face, then his dark eyes burned into hers.

'If that is what you wish,' he said, but there was a growl just beneath the words. 'Although it would be advisable for both of us to reside in the same place so Peter Richards's lawyers do not see this as a sham.'

'You can live in my apartment—there's a spare bedroom,' Marty offered, mentally clearing away the office paraphernalia and assorted junk she kept in there, to divert her body from its excited frolic at the thought of Carlos living so close.

'So you will do it? I will ask Lisa to arrange the papers and bring them to us for our signatures. Would tonight be too soon?'

The end of the world would be too soon, but Marty thought of Emmaline and nodded.

'You may as well move in straight away—save hotel expenses. Lawyers don't come cheap and it seems the fight could go on for some years.'

'I do not need to worry about such things,' he replied, 'but I thank you for the thought. I am not reliant on wages for my income, but have family businesses and property, so I promise you will not be out of pocket at all.'

Marty waved away the final phrase, her mind picking up on the earlier part of his statement.

'You have money? A lot of money?' she demanded, and though Carlos looked taken aback by the urgency of her questions, he nodded.

'Enough,' he said, and Marty shook her head.

'*That* explains it!' she said. 'I've been puzzling over why Peter Richards would want Emmaline, but it's for the same reason Natalie kept the baby—for money—your money. Did Natalie know you were wealthy?'

Carlos smiled, but cynicism twisted any humour out of the expression.

'How could she help but know, living as she did in my family home in Barcelona, a home she thought a palace, it is so large, and visiting our other estates? Having accounts at all the best stores? Oh, yes, Natalie knew!'

'So if Peter gets custody of Emmaline, he can apply to the courts to be awarded both child support for her, plus whatever settlement you might have made to Natalie on your divorce. I looked him up on the internet and all his schemes have involved making money in some way. If he had Emmaline, he could milk you for the rest of his life— and you would never know if the money was being spent on her or not.'

'I would know!' Carlos said, his voice so deep and determined Marty shivered. 'But it is not an issue,' he continued, in the same grave tones. 'He will *not* get Emmaline!'

The commitment and determination in his voice told Marty she had made the right decision. She, too, was doing this for Emmaline, and if later she suffered heartache, at least she'd have the satisfaction of knowing the child she loved would not grow up with someone as amoral in his dealings as Peter Richards.

'You will not eat more?'

Carlos waved his hand towards the plates left untouched in the centre of the table.

'The sandwiches I tried tasted like sawdust and the coffee worse than usual for canteen coffee,' Marty told him, then checked her watch.

'I should go back to work. I'm due off duty at five but

who knows if that will be the case? Do you want a key to my apartment so you can move in whenever it suits you?'

Carlos studied her for a moment, then a little smile stretched his lips.

'So cool and practical,' he teased. 'Are you sure a marriage of convenience—by which I read platonic—is what you want, Marty Cox? Are you really so adept at controlling the fires that burn inside you that you don't want us to give and take of love while we are together?'

'It would be sex, not love,' Marty reminded him, hiding her secret deep within her heart.

'But cannot that provide solace and comfort as well as considerable pleasure for us both? Should we deny ourselves even that?'

Should they?

Her body told her exactly how it felt about the situation. Even sitting here with Carlos, it yearned to feel his touch and brush against his skin and fit its curves to his hardness.

But how much harder the parting would be if she allowed it to happen—if she got used to having Carlos in her bed, then had to get used to emptiness again.

'I'm marrying you for Emmaline,' she reminded him, which wasn't really answering the question at all...

CHAPTER TEN

MARTY returned to her ward, checking first on Summer, who was still in Theatre, but once back at work she found her hands were shaking so badly she sought refuge in her office, telling staff she'd be there if needed but that she had a mass of paperwork to tackle so would prefer not to be disturbed.

She should calm down, but the enormity of her decision had her rattled and although she continued to tell herself this marriage would mean nothing, she couldn't hide a whisper of excitement from creating havoc in her body.

'Patients first,' she reminded herself, pulling Regan Collins's file from a pile on her desk. She had a letter to write to the girl's GP and a routine follow-up call to make. Maybe talking to Ms Collins might calm her down.

'Regan's fine,' Ms Collins told her. 'As you suggested, I'm keeping her off school for a few days—in fact, we're both discussing other options as far as school's concerned. My parents are getting older and would like me to move closer to them, and Regan loves her grandparents and has friends in the country town where they live, so maybe this was what we needed to prompt us to make some big changes in our lives.'

Tell me about it! Marty wanted to say, but instead she

expressed her pleasure that all was well and listened for a while longer while Ms Collins elaborated on their tentative plans.

'I stayed in Brisbane because Regan's dad was here, but he hardly ever sees her, so what's the point?'

I know how that is too, Marty thought, although now she began to wonder about Emmaline's dad. Would he always want to see her?

Would he stay married to her, if only in name, so he stayed in his daughter's life?

And was that what she wanted—a sham marriage?

A long-term rather than a temporary sham?

No, nothing would be better than that.

'Thanks for phoning,' Ms Collins said at last. 'And thanks for all you did and the comfort you gave Regan. She knows she did a very stupid thing, and that she's lucky there'll be no long-term consequences. You're the best!'

The compliment eased some of Marty's troubled thoughts, but as she lifted the phone to ring Theatre and check again on Summer, trouble walked back through the door.

'I'm leaving now,' Carlos said. 'I've explained to the A and E supervisor that I need some time over the next few days for personal business and I've arranged a meeting with Lisa at five.'

He hesitated, seeming ill at ease for the first time since Marty had met him.

'You mentioned a key?'

'You want to move in today?'

She wasn't sure why this was upsetting her when, in fact, she'd suggested it—although that had been back when she'd thought him an impoverished doctor working for his keep in Africa.

'If it still suits you it might be best, as there will be matters we need to discuss and papers to sign, and with working hours, it could be difficult for us to be together.'

Marty pulled her little backpack out of her bottom drawer and found her coin purse where she kept a spare apartment key for times when she mislaid her main keyring.

But handing over the key was hard—not only because it would mean finger contact with a man who, just standing there, could fire her blood, but also because jealousy now gnawed within her. Just how late would he be to need to use the key after his five o'clock meeting with Lisa?

With Lisa, who'd offered to marry him?

For legal reasons, of course!

She flipped the key across to him, watching as he caught it in one hand, then he smiled and all her good intentions about not revealing her feelings in front of this man melted to nothingness.

She smiled back, though when he tossed the key in the air and caught it once again, saying, 'So we shall be roomies? Is that not right?' she had to fight the excitement the words conjured up.

'Roomies share a room—we're flatmates,' she told him, and if he was disappointed by her reply, she couldn't tell, for the smile was gone and the mask firmly back in place.

He said goodbye and departed, though he did phone her later to enquire about Summer, who was by then in Recovery. His backpack was sitting on the bed in the spare room when Marty arrived home after waiting at the hospital until Summer had regained consciousness and the surgeon had announced he was cautiously optimistic she would suffer no ill effects from the tumour.

Working around the single piece of luggage—why

wouldn't she have supposed he was an impoverished doctor?—she cleared her things out of the room, tidied the rest of the apartment, went down to the local shop to restock the pantry and refrigerator, and was about to luxuriate in a bath before bed when she was called to the hospital.

She left a note for Carlos, telling him to help himself to food and explaining where she was going and why—a post-partum haemorrhage requiring surgery and the obstetrician on duty needing a second pair of hands in Theatre.

Looking back on that night a week later, Marty realised it had set the pattern for their life together. If she was at home, Carlos wasn't, and if he was in the apartment, she was, not always by choice, absent from it. They met at times, both there and at the hospital, often both visiting Emmaline at the same time, the ban on Carlos visiting having now lifted, thanks to Lisa's efforts.

'We have to stop meeting like this,' he said, late on Tuesday afternoon in the NICU, and Marty smiled to think there must be a similar cliché in Spanish that he would use it.

'I've been busy,' she said, although she knew she'd made herself keep busy to avoid too much time together.

'And I,' he said, 'but tonight there are no meetings with lawyers or duty for you, I believe. Could I take you out to dinner? Is that allowable for flatmates?'

The pain in Marty's bruised heart eased immediately, and her body tingled with excitement.

It's dinner, for heaven's sake, she told it, but the tingling didn't stop.

'That would be nice,' she said, hoping the bland description would hide her excitement.

'You will suggest where?'

'There's a restaurant at the eastern end of the river walk where we can sit outside. It's lovely at this time of year.'

Carlos nodded, then, as the nurse settled a sleeping Emmaline back into her crib, he took Marty's arm and steered her out of the ward.

'You are through work? We can walk home together?'

Marty couldn't help but remember the last time they'd done that, and the aftermath of it, but she nodded, perhaps needing to walk home with Carlos, to make things comfortable between them before they went through with their strange—and probably strained—wedding ceremony the following Saturday.

So once again they walked beneath the arch of bougainvillea, Carlos's hand gripping her elbow, her body falling into rhythm with his while it heated from the contact.

'The original of my marriage certificate with Natalie has arrived and as a legal search has found no evidence of her filing divorce papers, Lisa is certain we will get custody of Emmaline, at least while the case is fought.'

This reminder of his marriage to the beautiful woman, and the mention of the lawyer who'd offered to marry him, cooled Marty enough to remember exactly what was going on here. This was not a courtship, but a business arrangement. It depressed her so much she couldn't even feel pleased about the Emmaline news, although she did feel comforted by it.

'When will she know?' Marty asked, deciding it was time to stop thinking about herself and get with the conversation.

'She cannot take it further until Peter Richards makes his move. As she explains it, our position is that there is no doubt Emmaline is my—soon to be our—child, so we have no need to apply for custody. He must make his claim to the court, and when that happens we will counter it.'

'Maybe he won't,' Marty said, then she stopped as the real import of his words struck home. 'And if he doesn't, there's no need for us to get married,' she added, turning so she could look into Carlos's face. 'We'd be jumping the gun here. He might not file a claim. The letter might have been a try-on, just to see how you'd react.'

Carlos studied her, his eyes scanning her face.

'You would take that risk? With Emmaline?'

An image of the baby flashed through Marty's mind—the tiny, helpless child, caught in this web of greed.

'No,' she said soberly. 'I wouldn't.'

Carlos took her elbow once again, and their bodies brushed together as they walked, but the fires were diminished now—overwhelmed by thoughts of all that lay ahead.

A shower helped wash away her gloom, then putting on the dress she'd bought while with him made her feel a million dollars. Forget it all for one stolen night of pleasure, she ordered herself. Go out, have fun, eat well and enjoy the company of the man you…

She couldn't think the word—not now—not when it would be so easy to reveal just how she felt.

'You look wonderful,' he said, when she came lightly into the living room to find him in the black silk polo shirt and black slacks he'd been wearing the day he dived into the river.

'You don't look so bad yourself,' she told him, then asked if he'd like a drink.

'You are not on call? You can have one with me?'

Marty nodded.

'Then the drinks are on me. I found a place that sells Spanish wine and amazingly enough it had some that comes from one of our vineyards. I have it in the refrigerator, cooling, in the hope that you might like to try it.'

Marty smiled, having learnt by now that his language became more formal when he was a little uncertain about a situation. That he, too, felt uncertain about the evening ahead made her feel enormously better.

'A toast!' he said, returning with two brimming glasses. '*Salud.*'

He touched his glass to hers, and Marty lifted hers to sip the pale liquid.

'It's delicious. Dry yet slightly sweet. May I see the bottle?'

'You read Spanish now?' Carlos teased.

'I'm hoping grapes have recognisable names in any language,' she told him, then took the bottle, moisture beading on its surface, from his hands.

The label had a picture of a castle on a hill, with grape vines stretching down and away from it. The name, Quintero, was clear enough but the rest of it—well, no, she couldn't read Spanish.

But the castle?

'That's just a picture, isn't it?' she asked, pointing to the impressive edifice.

'It is my favourite place on earth,' he said quietly. 'Were we marrying in Spain we would be honeymooning there.'

'We're not honeymooning anywhere,' Marty reminded him. 'It's not that kind of marriage.'

Then she realised that wasn't the point. If Carlos or his family owned the castle, there were other things to be sorted out.

'Is it yours?' she asked, and saw him shrug.

'It is—mine alone—for it came into the family through

my grandmother who loved it as I love it. She was able to leave it where she wished, and she left it to me.'

He took Marty's free hand and looked down into her face.

'I have always felt, when I can no longer work in places like Africa, that I would like to live there permanently. Natalie, of course, hated the idea, as it is far away from the big cities she loved so much. But there's a village there and we are not far from Toledo, where you could practise if you wanted to work…'

Marty frowned at him.

At the way he was talking…

She sipped her wine, slid her hand away from his and walked away, out to the balcony where she watched the river flow quietly by.

She sensed him coming, felt him join her, as if her body was attuned to all his movements.

'Marty?'

She couldn't face him—not while she asked.

'Carlos…' she began, but her voice faltered on his name and she had to start again, but looking at him now, watching his face, needing to see his reaction.

'Carlos, you talk as if this marriage will continue,' she managed—no reaction to see. 'As if it's for real and will go on past whatever time it needs to ensure Emmaline is safely yours.'

Dark eyes studied her intently and she met his gaze but couldn't guess what he was thinking.

'You have not considered this? You want it to be a temporary thing? Dissolved when Emmaline is safe?'

Why's he asking?

Does he *want* to be married to me?

And why would he want that, when he owns castles and

vineyards and could be married to a princess or a super-model or someone as fabulously wealthy as he obviously is?

None of it made sense, and she wasn't sure asking him these questions would make a difference. He had a way of answering without answering—so she was left more be-fuddled than she'd been before she'd asked.

'I don't know what I want!' she told him helplessly, then she remembered what she'd been about to say when she'd learnt he owned the castle in the picture. 'And what I want isn't the issue right now. I don't know if you've thought of it, but nowhere among the papers we've signed has there been a prenuptial agreement.'

'You want a prenuptial agreement? Are you talking of a paper signed that designates what you get if the marriage does not last? Is it for this you are marrying me?'

He sounded so genuinely upset she touched his arm, but she had to smile as she explained.

'Not what I get,' she explained, 'but what I don't get. When I thought I was marrying Carlos, the doctor from Sudan, it wasn't important, but surely your lawyer, either the one here or the one in Spain, has told you that you can't go into marriage without securing your assets. Didn't you do this with Natalie? Didn't your lawyer insist?'

Carlos moved away—his turn to look out at the river.

'We did sign an agreement,' he said quietly, 'but as she hadn't filed for divorce, it doesn't count in the situation in which we now find ourselves.'

He turned back to face Marty.

'I had thought you were different—that we would not need such a piece of paper.'

His voice was cold but Marty still heard the distress in it. She put down her glass and went to stand in front of him, slipping her arms around his waist and looking up into his stern face.

'We need a piece of paper for you,' she said softly. 'A piece that says I neither want nor should get a thing out of this marriage. Visiting rights to Emmaline is something we can work out, but I was thinking of you, Carlos, and the protection of all you hold dear, when I suggested we should sign something.'

His face lightened and a smile glimmered in his eyes, but he shook his head in disbelief then put his arms around her and drew her close.

'You can have the lot, as far as I'm concerned,' he whispered to her. 'You are unbelievable—that you could do so much for me then ask for nothing.'

He rocked her against him and without warning— though she should have known—all the embers she'd banked down inside her flared back to life, and desire, rich and hot and urgent, ricocheted through her body.

'We'd better eat,' he said, and the thickness in his voice told her he felt the same way.

'We'd better,' she whispered, but remained where she was, so Carlos had to disentangle the two of them, setting her away from him, kissing her briefly on the lips before taking her glass inside and putting the bottle of wine back into the refrigerator.

'Come,' he ordered, picking up her little backpack and handing it to her. 'We shall walk and eat and then walk home and at that time discuss the success, advisability and impossibilities of platonic marriages.'

Marty felt her body heat again and she smiled as she shook her head at him.

'You don't think they work?'

He smiled back.

'Not for us,' he said softly.

And the tingling excitement she'd tried so hard to quell became a rushing whirlwind that made her knees tremble and her heart pound erratically.

But Carlos was insistent they go out to eat, so the excitement was tucked away, although it simmered strongly enough for her to react to every touch and gesture, even to his voice, as they walked and talked of other things—of Summer and her baby Wind Cloud, of Emmaline and her future, and of Regan Collins, Marty passing on the news that she and her mother were thinking of relocating so they would be closer to Ms Collins's parents.

'You would miss your mother if you moved away?' Carlos asked, and Marty, considering the change in circumstances in her relationship with her mother, hesitated before replying.

'Two weeks ago my answer would have been different. I'd have said I wouldn't move away—wouldn't work elsewhere for any extended length of time—because of her,' she admitted. 'Not because she'd have stopped me, or even from some sense of duty, but I owe her so much, Carlos, that to hurt her by moving somewhere else permanently, well, I couldn't do it—not unless she'd have been willing to come with me.'

'And now?'

'Now she has Alec, it's different. She has a new life and although I'll always be part of it, and she'll always be part of mine, maybe she'll be the one to move away—certainly she's free to do that—but whatever happens, it's wonderful.'

They walked on, arriving at the restaurant, Carlos not asking further questions and Marty realising they'd been prompted by her talk of Regan's future, not because he was intent on whisking her, Marty, away to castles in Spain or war-torn African countries.

'Though Africa would be nice,' she muttered to herself, as Carlos and the restaurant manager discussed which table they would take. 'A safe part of Africa because of Emmaline...'

Replete with good food—also of Africa, Marty having forgotten when she mentioned the restaurant that it specialised in Moroccan food—they walked back to the apartment, not talking much, content to be together, the simmering excitement building for, even without the discussion Carlos had promised, they both knew the platonic part of the relationship was over.

'This time we will make love in bed,' Carlos announced as they walked into the hallway and turned to kiss. 'It will be our first time there and therefore special, and I will show you I have more than castles to offer you.'

He lifted her, as he did so effortlessly, and carried her into the bedroom, setting her on her feet this time, then drawing her dress over her head with slow deliberation.

Glad she'd bought the new underwear, she stood, transfixed by his inspection of her, excited by the smile that widened on his lips.

'You denigrate yourself, *querida*, when you talk of being plain and wear those concealing clothes. You have a body all women would envy, a body to worship, not to hide.'

And with hands and lips he showed her what he meant until she demanded fair time and stripped off his clothes, touching him as he'd touched her, pressing her lips against his skin, teasing him until he shook with need, and lifted her again, this time to toss her on the bed and make her his, growling beneath his breath while she cried out her satisfaction.

They slept, limbs tangled in the tumbled bedclothes and woke to love again, Marty determined to set all doubts about what lay ahead aside and live for the moment, enjoying the sheer bliss of being Carlos's lover and revelling in the obvious enjoyment she gave to him.

But life had a way of intruding on bliss and two nights later Carlos greeted her not with a hug and a kiss but with a strained smile and an absent-minded peck on the cheek.

'What's wrong?' Marty demanded, dumping her back-pack on a chair and looking up into his face.

'Peter Richards has launched his claim.'

Marty put her arms around him, and felt tension in every sinew of his body.

'It's not so bad,' she murmured. 'No more than we expected. It's why we're getting married, remember.'

Carlos stepped from her imprisoning arms.

'I don't like that you think that way!' he snapped, puzzling Marty totally until he added, as if the two were linked, 'The court has ordered DNA tests because of what he claims.'

Ah! The dreaded DNA question that Carlos had been dodging and she'd been avoiding asking.

She followed him to where he stood beside the glass door to the balcony, and stood close, although he'd repudiated closeness earlier.

'Why is that so bad, Carlos?' she asked. 'And this time I want an answer—not a kiss to divert me or some other subject raised. Why are you so bothered by the thought of DNA tests?'

He looked down at her and for the first time since they had met she read what looked like real pain in his eyes.

'Suppose she is not mine?' he whispered. 'And not being mine, I would have no claim to keep her from that grasping, no-good man? Suppose she is not mine, when I have grown to love her, Marty?'

His voice broke on her name and she put her arms around him once again, pulling his head down onto her shoulder so she could comfort him while he let out his grief.

'Of course she's yours,' she told him as he straightened up again, not adding that she couldn't imagine anyone who'd been to bed with Carlos ever wanting to be with anyone else.

But he wasn't to be comforted by empty assurances and shook his head, leading Marty to the couch and easing her down—sitting beside her with his hand holding hers.

'You, who are all that is honourable and good, would think that, but Natalie was different. She was beautiful and determined and perhaps you would say wilful. I had to be away at times, a two-day trip to Paris to see the people for whom I work, trips to the country estates to see the tenants and talk business with my managers. She had ample opportunity to take other lovers, Marty, and I knew that at the time, and suspected she might do it, if only to punish me for leaving her and to taunt me with her behaviour.'

'Oh, Carlos!'

Marty nestled into him, unable to believe the pain such suspicions must have caused him, and the agony he'd been through since he'd seen the child that might, or might not, be his. 'This is why you didn't want the test earlier?'

He nodded, but said nothing, and although she searched her head and heart there was nothing she could say—no solace she could offer him.

Or was there?

Not solace exactly, but surely it could warm him slightly.

She eased out the secret she'd tucked away in her heart, and mentally checked it out, viewing it from all angles before releasing it into the air.

'I love you, Carlos,' she whispered. 'I know that doesn't help, and that you really didn't want my love, but it's there, and it's yours, for whatever it's worth.'

He held her close, then kissed her, and they comforted each other in the way they both knew best.

'It's not love, you know,' Marty murmured to Sophie, who was fiddling with a tiny coronet of rosebuds she'd made for Marty's hair.

'Tell that to the mirror,' Sophie told her. 'It *might* believe you, although, seeing the stars in the eyes of that reflection, I doubt it would.'

'I'm marrying him for legal reasons—to make sure we can keep Emmaline while everything is sorted out. It's a marriage of convenience and this getting all dressed up is really silly.'

Or so it felt, now the time had come, for not once since she'd told Carlos of her love had he mentioned it. But she was getting dressed up for her mother, who believed in love, not Carlos, she reminded herself, as Sophie gave the coronet a final tweak.

They were in the bedroom of the flat at Sophie and Gib's house, getting ready for a hastily arranged marriage that was to take place in the garden by the river in twenty minutes' time. Not wishing to upset her mother by explaining the true circumstances of the wedding, Marty had agreed to do things properly, going back to Ellen's boutique and buying one of the dresses Carlos had liked, a pale silvery green like the leaves of a wattle tree that fitted her bust and waist then flared out with panels that floated as she moved, some short enough to show a glimpse of thigh while others reached mid-calf.

And true to tradition, she'd spent the previous night not in Carlos's arms but in her old bedroom at her mother's house, her mother bringing her breakfast in bed, so excited at her daughter's wedding her hands shook as she poured the tea. Lucy had helped her dress, then she and Alec had driven her to Sophie and Gib's.

'Does he believe this marriage of convenience talk?' Sophie asked.

'He suggested it,' Marty said, and then she blushed, thinking how far from platonic their relationship had become.

'Oh, yes!' Sophie, perhaps seeing the blush, teased.

Marty said nothing, because she knew things hadn't changed between them. Well, in bed they had, but not in other ways. Although she'd told Carlos of her love for him, the circumstances of the marriage remained the same— they were marrying for Emmaline, to safeguard the future of the tiny girl they both loved.

But once that was done?

It was a question she'd refused to consider as she'd made her preparations for this day. Carlos might talk as if their future lay together, but to tie him to her for ever when he didn't love her?

Could she do that to him?

Was it fair? Particularly when he would carry the burden of knowing she loved him.

Love was a responsibility and Carlos was a man who took responsibility seriously!

Panic rioted in her chest and though she knew her

mother and Alec were already there, waiting with the marriage celebrant down at the gazebo, and Gib would be standing by Carlos, ready to act as best man, she wanted nothing more than to run away.

'I can't do it,' she said, clutching Sophie's arm, her fingers biting into her friend's flesh.

A knock came on the door, and Sophie went to answer it, speaking in a low voice, protesting, until Marty heard the other person answer and knew that it was Carlos.

'I must see her,' he was insisting, explaining this was not a normal marriage and such stupid customs as not seeing the bride had no place in it. Then he was there, shutting Sophie outside and coming towards Marty with his hands outstretched.

He clasped hers and held them, looking down at her, enough appreciation in his eyes to make her glad she'd bought the dress—a strange thought when her entire being was poised for flight.

But when he spoke it wasn't to compliment her on her appearance, but rather to reassure her, as if, by instinct, he'd known of her sudden fear.

'We've had no time together lately,' he said quietly, then to her surprise he blushed. 'Not sensible time,' he amended. 'Time out of bed in which to talk. Last night, alone with my thoughts for company, I realised I hadn't told you just how much this means to me—that you would do this for me and my daughter.'

He squeezed her hands and gave a strained laugh.

'I find it hard to say all this when all I want to do is hold you in my arms and hug you tight, but you look so beautiful I would surely crush the lovely dress and squash the rosebuds in your hair, so I must hold back and try to express my thanks, Marty, in inadequate words and in a tongue that is not my own.'

'There's no need for thanks,' Marty managed, although her heart was beating so hard it was a wonder she could speak. 'We both know why we're doing this.'

He nodded, and stepped back, but seemed reluctant to release her hands.

'I must go,' he said, 'for Sophie is outraged by my impropriety, but—'

'But what, Carlos?'

'I have a gift for you, something I wish to give you before we wed, not after.'

A wedding ring—no, he'd be giving her that later, as she'd be giving one to him.

'There's nothing in your hands,' she pointed out when he hesitated so long she thought she'd burst with curiosity.

'It isn't in my hands but in my heart,' he said. 'In fact, it is my heart, which I now give to you.'

He reached out his hands as if they held a gift and handed it to her, then took the hands she'd held out to receive it.

'Keep it safe for me, *querida*, for it has had a long journey before it found a safe haven. I have fancied myself in love before, but until I found and felt the magnitude of what you feel for me, I didn't understand it—didn't know it could exist like that.'

He raised her hands to his lips and kissed each fingertip.

'You do not want my castles but will you take my heart? My love? My very self?'

He stood before her, trembling slightly, and she knew he spoke the truth—and that this was the greatest gift a man could give a woman on her wedding day.

CHAPTER ELEVEN

MARRIED life was wonderful, Marty decided as she all but skipped along the path towards her apartment, thinking of Carlos there with Emmaline, and the news he'd phoned through that day.

Three whole weeks and they were still in love. Tired the last few days because a certain demanding young lady had come home from hospital and two-hourly feeds meant neither of them got much sleep, but the joy of having Emmie home was worth the sleepless nights, and the delight at watching her feed and move and sometimes smile more than made up for lack of sleep.

Carlos must have heard her key in the lock as he was coming towards her as she opened the door. He took her in his arms and kissed her deeply.

'She's just gone down to sleep, we have two hours—you are tired after your day?'

She met his kiss with all the passion that surged inside her—a passion not spent as often these days with a tiny intruder in the house. 'Never too tired for you,' she whispered in the kiss.

'Then we shall celebrate our child,' he announced, going to the refrigerator and bringing out a bottle of champagne.

He waved it aloft, then grabbed two glasses. 'In the bedroom, no?'

Marty followed him, only too glad to join the celebrations, for today they'd heard that the DNA results had proved Emmaline was indeed his child. Peter Richards might continue to fight, but the legal opinions were that he would lose.

Carlos opened the bottle and poured them each a drink, while Marty showered before joining him in the bedroom. He handed her a glass, and toasted her, then kissed her while her lips were still wet with the wine.

'I love you, Marty Quintero,' he told her, as he did a hundred times each day, but then he added more. 'I did try not to, because I'd loved foolishly once before, and felt that love had cheated me, but this was different love, that comes from inside the heart, and grows and grows.'

Overwhelmed to hear this reserved man open up like this, Marty set down her glass and took him in her arms and told him of her love in other ways.

Later, as they lay at ease together, Marty nestled against his body, Carlos ran his fingers through her hair, then turned so he was facing her.

'Today I phoned a friend in France,' he said, and her heart stood still. For all his talk of love, would he leave her to go back to Africa?

And could she blame him, knowing how much the work he did there meant to him?

'He had offered me a job once before—with a children's health organisation—in Botswana.'

'Botswana!' Marty breathed, tasting the magical name on her tongue and wondering about exotic places.

'Botswana is safe,' Carlos said, and Marty realised his

voice had become tentative, as if he was uncertain how to go on.

She propped herself on one elbow and looked down into his face, her finger tracing the outline of his lips.

'How safe?' she demanded, and he smiled—but still tentatively.

'Safe enough for me to take a wife and child. There is work there for another doctor, especially one with your skills, for it is through the women we will have to work to get the vaccination programme going. There is a house, with staff to look after us and help with Emmie while we work. There is clean water and power, most of the time, and a need for doctors but no war.'

'You want me to come?' Marty asked, unable to believe it could be possible.

'How could I go without you?' Carlos said simply, then he wrapped his arms around her and hugged her hard, whispering the explanation in her ear. 'You who are the better part of me—my breath, my heart, my life?'

Could dreams really become reality? Marty wondered. Could it really be that she could travel to these places, and have this precious child, and be loved so much? Could this have happened?

'It is my dream for us to do this together,' Carlos added. 'You will come?'

Marty shifted, then pressed a kiss on his lips.

'I will come,' she told him. And in that moment, she knew all of her dreams really had come true.

MILLS & BOON®

Live the emotion

_Medical
romance™

A FATHER BEYOND COMPARE
by *Alison Roberts*

When paramedic Tom Gardiner rescued single mum Emma and her young son, he didn't realise that by saving their lives he'd changed his own forever... He'd thought he never wanted a family, but with Emma and little Mickey around Tom's life was beginning to change. Could he convince Emma that her past belonged in the past and her future lay with him?

AN UNEXPECTED PROPOSAL *by Amy Andrews*

GP Madeline Harrington makes it very clear to her new neighbour Dr Marcus Hunt that she doesn't like his approach to medicine – and doesn't like him! But as Marcus's healing touch gradually wins her over, Madeline realises that she might have misjudged this very brilliant, very gorgeous doctor...

SHEIKH SURGEON, SURPRISE BRIDE
by *Josie Metcalfe*

Ambitious orthopaedic surgeon Lily Langley is delighted to be working with the prestigious Razak Khan! Lily is not prepared for the rush of sensual heat that sparks between them every time their eyes meet... Razak is attracted to Lily, but he has duties that will take him back to his desert kingdom, away from this English beauty...

On sale 2nd March 2007

Available at WHSmith, Tesco, ASDA, and all good bookshops
www.millsandboon.co.uk

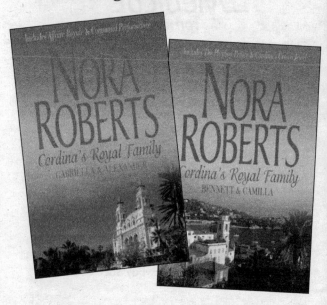

FREE

4 BOOKS AND A SURPRISE GIFT!

We would like to take this opportunity to thank you for reading this Mills & Boon® book by offering you the chance to take FOUR more specially selected titles from the Medical Romance™ series absolutely FREE! We're also making this offer to introduce you to the benefits of the Mills & Boon® Reader Service™—

* ★ FREE home delivery
* ★ FREE gifts and competitions
* ★ FREE monthly Newsletter
* ★ Books available before they're in the shops
* ★ Exclusive Reader Service offers

Accepting these FREE books and gift places you under no obligation to buy; you may cancel at any time, even after receiving your free shipment. Simply complete your details below and return the entire page to the address below. You don't even need a stamp!

YES! Please send me 4 free Medical Romance books and a surprise gift. I understand that unless you hear from me, I will receive 6 superb new titles every month for just £2.80 each, postage and packing free. I am under no obligation to purchase any books and may cancel my subscription at any time. The free books and gift will be mine to keep in any case.

M7ZEE

Ms/Mrs/Miss/Mr...Initials ....
BLOCK CAPITALS PLEASE

Surname ....

Address ....

....

....Postcode ....

Send this whole page to:

The Reader Service, FREEPOST CN81, Croydon, CR9 3WZ